ADVANCE PRAISE FOR *DRAGON MOUNTAIN*:

"DRAGON MOUNTAIN has all of my favorite things! A rich mythology and a tale of friendship, snarky dragons, and daring deeds . . . this is the kind of breathless tale that leaves you hungry for the next installment."
—Roshani Chokshi, *New York Times* bestselling author of *Aru Shah and the End of Time*

"Brimming with warmth and originality, DRAGON MOUNTAIN combines edge-of-your-seat adventure, laugh-out-loud humor, and hugely exciting dragons to create a sweeping fantasy that will captivate readers of all ages."—Catherine Doyle, author of The Storm Keeper's Island series

PRAISE FOR KATIE & KEVIN TSANG'S SAM WU SERIES:

PRAISE FOR *SAM WU IS NOT AFRAID OF GHOSTS*:

"Reluctant readers and fans of the Wimpy Kid series and its ilk will appreciate the book's dynamic type, graphics galore, cartoonish illustrations, and ironic footnotes."—*Kirkus*

"Fans of Alvin Ho and Hank Zipzer will laugh out loud at Sam's zany capers."
—*School Library Journal*

"Sam is an everykid, trying to fit in, hoping he can become braver, and determined to outsmart his nemesis, Ralph, which is difficult, but not impossible. A quick read for young middle-graders."—*Booklist Online*

PRAISE FOR *SAM WU IS NOT AFRAID OF SHARKS:*

"An engaging and authentic underdog tale that fans of Mark Parisi's 'Marty Pants' and Lenore Look's 'Alvin Ho' series will enjoy."—*School Library Journal*

" . . . will attract readers, particularly, perhaps, reluctant ones."—*Booklist*

"This second installment . . . should find its readers, who may find comfort and confidence in following Sam's incremental growth. . . . A sequel . . . finds its way."—*Kirkus*

DRAGON MOUNTAIN

BY KATIE & KEVIN TSANG

FOR EVIE, OUR BABY DRAGON.

STERLING CHILDREN'S BOOKS
New York

An Imprint of Sterling Publishing Co., Inc.
122 Fifth Avenue
New York, NY 10011

ISBN 978-1-4549-3596-4
ISBN 978-1-4549-3597-1 (e-book)

Distributed in Canada by Sterling Publishing Co., Inc.
$^{c}/_{o}$ Canadian Manda Group, 664 Annette Street
Toronto, Ontario M6S 2C8, Canada
Distributed in the United Kingdom by GMC Distribution Services
Castle Place, 166 High Street, Lewes, East Sussex BN7 1XU, England
Distributed in Australia by NewSouth Books
University of New South Wales, Sydney, NSW 2052, Australia

For information about custom editions, special sales, and premium and
corporate purchases, please contact Sterling Special Sales at 800-805-5489
or specialsales@sterlingpublishing.com.

Manufactured in the United States of America

Lot #:
2 4 6 8 10 9 7 5 3 1
09/20

sterlingpublishing.com

Design by Julie Robine

DRAGON MOUNTAIN

BY KATIE & KEVIN TSANG

STERLING CHILDREN'S BOOKS
New York

CHAPTER 1
THE MOUNTAIN

Mountains always have secrets.

And this one had more than most. Tall and majestic, with jagged peaks that punctured the sky, it appeared unknowable and immovable.

And yet, if you were to watch it and not just glance at it—really watch it—it would sometimes appear to be breathing.

If you stared long enough, you'd start to think that it was a different mountain altogether.

One person had been watching this mountain for a very, very long time.

And he had decided it was time for the mountain to show him its secrets.

Deep within the mountain, a great creature stirred in its sleep. Its eyes rolled back in its head, and its wings jerked wide open. It suddenly sat straight up, trying to remember what it had seen in the nightmare.

Darkness. All it saw was darkness and desolation.

The creature shuddered and closed its eyes, trying to go back to sleep.

It had been waiting for something, for someone, for a long time. It could wait longer.

CHAPTER 2
ARRIVAL

Billy Chan was certain of two things. He had great hair, and he was the best surfer in the eleven-to-fourteen age bracket in all of California.

He did not think either of those things was going to help him in his current situation. He was by himself. On a train platform. Somewhere in middle-of-nowhere China. The train ride had felt like forever. He didn't even know what time it was. He reached into his pocket and gripped his lucky seashell. At least he had a small piece of home with him.

All around him were huge mountains wrapped in green foliage climbing to dizzying heights. Even the Hong Kong skyscrapers he'd seen just a few days ago would have looked tiny here.

The only indication of *exactly* where in China he might be was written in peeling, faded yellow Chinese characters above the station doorway. Chinese characters that Billy couldn't read.

He really, really hoped he was in the right place.

Billy looked around, trying to find the promised staff of the summer camp he was going to. The summer camp his parents were forcing him to go to so he could "improve his Mandarin" and "learn more about his Chinese heritage." Even though what Billy *wanted* to do all summer was go surfing with his friends.

He did not see any camp staff. The only people nearby were two old Chinese women playing mahjong on a rickety table, cackling as they swirled the green tiles around.

"Hello?" he called out. "Ni-hao?"

One of the old women looked up and waved him toward the tiny station.

Billy nodded his thanks and went inside, dragging his suitcase behind him.

His eyes took a moment to adjust to the dim inside the station after the blisteringly bright sun outside. He breathed a sigh of relief. Clustered around the room were about a dozen kids his age.

A slightly older Chinese boy with slicked back black hair sauntered over holding a clipboard. He eyed Billy up and down, looking distinctly unimpressed.

"You must be Billy Chan," he said.

Billy nodded.

The boy sighed deeply, as if meeting Billy was the most annoying thing that had happened to him all day. "Finally," he said. "It took you long enough to get here."

Billy flushed. He was already off to a terrible start. "Well, this place is a *really* long way away from California. And my train was delayed . . ."

"Ni shuo putonghua ma?" the boy interrupted, his eyebrow raised.

Billy paused. He understood the boy was asking him if he spoke Mandarin, and he realized he had said this as a challenge.

"Yi dian dian," he replied, being careful to get his pronunciation right of the phrase meaning "a little bit."

The older boy frowned. "I guess you're not as Chinese as your name suggests, Billy *Chan*."

Billy was used to this. Used to people trying to figure out where he was from. He knew what the boy wanted to know. "My dad is Chinese. From Hong Kong. And my mom is white," he explained. "My parents sent me to this camp to improve my Mandarin." He tried to keep the bitterness out of his voice. He still hadn't forgiven his parents for making him spend his whole summer at a language culture camp in China. He looked at the other kids, who seemed to have gathered around them. "That's why we're all here, right?"

The responding nods and smiles made him feel slightly reassured.

"Whatever," said the older boy, sounding bored.

"And who are you?" said Billy, summoning as much confidence in his voice as he could muster.

The boy looked down his nose at Billy. "I'm JJ. My grandfather runs the camp."

"Got it, boss," said Billy, hoping JJ would pick up on

his sarcasm. Billy made a note to avoid him at all possible cost.

Just then, a wizened old Chinese man with a long white beard burst into the station, moving quickly, especially considering his age. He looked ancient, like he'd stepped out of the past.

"Welcome, everyone! I'm the head of camp. It is a pleasure to meet you all. You can call me Jin laoshi."

A short girl with long blond hair, almost to her waist, shot her hand up in the air. "As in 'Gold Teacher'?" She had a southern accent. Billy thought she must be from somewhere like Alabama.

The old man laughed. "Yes! I can tell someone already knows a bit of Mandarin."

Billy wished *he* had remembered that *laoshi* meant teacher. It was one of the first things he'd learned at Chinese school back home in San Francisco. He was hit by a wave of worry that everyone here was going to be better than he was. And, making things worse, the other students might expect him to be really good just because he was part Chinese. It didn't matter that his dad's side of the family was from Hong Kong and they spoke Cantonese, a different dialect of Chinese. He looked around at the eager faces of the other kids. They all seemed happy to be here. His palms started to sweat, and his neck felt hot. He wished he could jump back on the train and then a plane and go all the way home again.

"You can simply call me Lao Jin or Old Gold," the old man went on. "You aren't required to speak Mandarin outside of your language classes. But I'll explain all that when we get to camp. Now come with me," he said. "Our adventure is about to begin."

Billy followed Old Gold and the others into the parking lot, where a faded yellow and green van waited. Billy thought the car looked at least twice as old as him. Old Gold flung the door open, revealing two rows of six seats, like a miniature bus.

Billy climbed in and sat in the back. A boy with short brown hair, glasses, and more freckles than Billy had ever seen on anyone flopped into the seat next to him, breathing heavily.

"It is *hot* here," he said, wiping his brow. His green eyes were wide behind his glasses. "I'm Dylan O'Donnell, by the way." He stuck out his hand. Billy stared. He'd never seen someone his age introduce themselves with a handshake.

Billy blinked at the boy, trying to place his accent. It wasn't American, and it wasn't British, but it seemed strangely familiar.

"Um, hi. I'm Billy Chan," said Billy, awkwardly shaking Dylan's hand.

Nice to meet you! I've got a cousin named Billy," said Dylan, grinning as if this was a very interesting fact.

"Cool," said Billy. "Erm, I don't know anyone named Dylan."

"Pleasure to be the first!"

The van revved to life and, with a start, hurtled forward.

"Seatbelts, everyone!" shouted Old Gold from the front.

"So, where are you from?" asked Billy, still trying to place Dylan's accent.

"The Emerald Isle! Land of saints and scholars! Home of poets! And, yes, a lot of sheep." He said this last bit with a wry grin, like he was making a joke.

Billy stared at him, still confused. Dylan sighed.

"Ireland. I'm from Ireland."

Billy wracked his brain and tried to remember if he knew anything about Ireland. "Dublin?" he attempted.

"I'm from the west coast, actually. Galway. It's by the sea." Dylan's voice went up an octave as the van flew around a corner.

Billy's stomach churned as the van swayed, but he took a deep breath and tried to keep his cool. "Are you a surfer?" he asked Dylan, glad that his own voice stayed steady as the van took another wild turn.

Dylan laughed. He had a musical laugh, the kind you'd want to keep listening to long after it stopped.

"Me?" he said. "Oh, no. Too many jellyfish. And I sunburn easily, even in Ireland."

Billy tried to keep from visibly wilting. His suspicions about not having anything in common with the other kids at camp were right so far.

"Do *you* surf?" asked Dylan.

Billy nodded.

"Cowabunga, dude!" said Dylan in an atrocious American accent, making the hang loose sign with his left hand. He grinned, showing a gap between his two front teeth, and Billy found himself grinning back despite himself.

As they zoomed along narrow, winding roads, Old Gold rolled down the window and howled with glee.

Billy looked out the window, watching the world hurtle by. Amid flashes of green foliage and pockets of blue sky were glimpses of jagged yellow cliffs and stony peaks. Every time they swerved, he tensed, certain the van was going to tumble down into the ravine below.

He imagined the headline in the local news at home: "Local surf champion plummets to death in China." He bet his parents would be sorry then for sending him here all summer.

Dylan was clearly feeling the same way. "Going a bit fast, aren't we?" he said, looking panicked.

"My older brother likes to race cars," said a girl with long blond hair, the one who had known what laoshi meant. "So this is totally normal to me." Her pale face said otherwise. "I might even be a race-car driver one day."

"If we survive this journey, you mean," said Dylan, looking a little green.

Even though Billy had been thinking the exact same thing, he put on what he hoped was a reassuring smile. "I'm sure we're fine," he said.

Right then there was a thump and a scratch as a large branch hit the side of the van.

"Just a tree!" Old Gold hollered. "Nothing to worry about!"

The van whizzed on, higher and higher, and the landscape changed. Every bump in the road, and there were a lot, sent the van flying, giving Billy that same weightless feeling he got on roller coasters. They wound up and up until they were level with the clouds, and then . . .

"Whoa," breathed Billy. They were inside a cloud. All around them was a gray fog.

"I can't see anything!" screeched Dylan. "How can Old Gold see where he's going?"

"Don't worry," called Old Gold. "I can do this drive with my eyes closed!"

"Please don't!" Dylan cried back.

Old Gold just laughed.

They rumbled on, and with a sudden burst of sunshine, they were through the cloud cover and above it.

Billy was certain that if they went any higher they'd be able to touch the sky. In the distance he could see higher mountain peaks, their jagged points covered in snow.

"Is the camp on top of a cliff?" asked the blond girl.

"It's over this mountain," said JJ. "We're almost there."

The van zoomed down a steep incline, plunging them back into the cloud cover and then out again, but instead of jagged cliff faces, they were now surrounded by trees in every direction. Billy thought he glimpsed a waterfall, but they were going too fast for him to tell.

As the trees opened up into a clearing with a collection of small cabins scattered around, the van screeched to a stop, flinging them all forward against their seatbelts.

The van door slid open, showering them in sunlight.

"Welcome to Camp Dragon," said Old Gold.

CHAPTER 3
SOME THINGS CAN'T BE EXPLAINED

Beyond the cabins and tops of the trees stood a giant mountain watching over them. Billy tilted his head back so he could see the top. It was the biggest mountain he'd ever seen, and he felt small standing in its shadow.

In the distance Billy could hear rushing water and a sound he couldn't quite place. He waited a minute to make sure he wasn't imagining it. Yes, there it was again. A howling.

He could tell the instant Dylan heard it too, because his eyes got bigger and his mouth fell open.

"What *is* that?" asked Billy, looking around and trying to pinpoint the sound.

"Monkeys," said JJ, dropping their bags next to them. "They're everywhere around here. You'll get used to it."

"Monkeys?" Dylan exclaimed. "*Monkeys?*"

"Yes, monkeys. You know, long tail, small hands." JJ smirked. "Better watch out, some of them are as big as you. And they're fierce," he said over his shoulder as he went to get more bags out of the van.

Dylan paled. "Billy," he whispered. "I don't want to fight a monkey."

"Nobody is going to fight a monkey," Billy said, although he really had no idea. "And if we do, I'll take the first swing, okay?" He grinned at Dylan, trying to reassure him. Even though they'd just met, he could tell that Dylan was the kind of kid who was nervous about everything. But Billy didn't mind—having someone to reassure made him feel useful.

"All I know about monkeys is you shouldn't smile at them. Otherwise they'll think you're baring your teeth at them and will *attack!*" someone said with a southern accent. The blond girl appeared next to them, remarkably unwrinkled after their hair-raising bus journey. She bared her teeth at them. "Like this!"

"Got it," said Dylan. "Won't do that."

"Oh, excuse me, where are my manners?" she went on. "It is a pleasure to meet y'all. I'm Charlotte Bell, four-time winner of Little Miss of the South and two-time Jujitsu World Champion in the under-fourteen category." She curtsied.

Dylan and Billy stared at her. Then Dylan shrugged and gave an elaborate bow.

"Dylan O'Donnell, at your service."

Not to be outdone, Billy bowed too, a laugh bubbling up inside of him.

"I'm Billy Chan," he said. And then, with a sly smile he added, "And I've got multiple surf championship titles."

"Of course this camp is full of overachievers," moaned Dylan, but he was grinning. "I myself don't have any titles, although I did once come in second in a spelling bee."

"What is Little Miss of the South, anyway?" asked Billy.

"It's a pageant," Charlotte said, like it was obvious. "Where you have to have talents and stuff? That's why I'm so good at jujitsu, because it's my talent." She gave them a ferocious smile. "I bet I can beat both of you in an arm wrestle. Heck, I could flip both of you over right now."

"I believe you," Dylan said quickly, taking a small step back. "We'll take your word for it."

"Gather round, campers," called Old Gold, who was standing on top of a large tree stump. "Now I can formally welcome you to Camp Dragon! Let us all introduce ourselves."

Everyone formed a circle, saying their names and where they were from. Australia, Japan, India, Ghana, Denmark, France, England, and Argentina. Billy had never heard so many new accents before. There were fewer campers than he'd expected, though.

"What a wonderful sight to see all of you here for the inaugural year of Camp Dragon," said Old Gold. "Why, you might be asking, have I brought you so far from your homes to this place with log cabins and no internet? You twelve were brought to my attention by someone in your life who knows you very well—a teacher, a librarian, a coach. I sent out a call to my colleagues around the world for twelve of the best and brightest, and you all are it."

"Excuse me," said Charlotte, raising her hand. "There are only eleven of us, not twelve."

"Congratulations, you know how to count," said JJ drolly. Charlotte glared at him.

"Well noticed, Charlotte," said Old Gold. "I can tell you have a keen eye. You are correct."

"I wouldn't have said it if it wasn't correct," said Charlotte with a degree of self-confidence bordering on cockiness. Billy was both a little bit in awe and alarmed. She seemed like the kind of person who was very used to getting her way, no matter what. He definitely didn't want to get on her bad side.

Old Gold cleared his throat. "Yes, well, as I was saying, you have all been brought here for a special reason."

"Is he the twelfth person?" Charlotte interrupted again, pointing at JJ.

Dylan buried his face in his hands. "Please, in the name of all that is holy, as my nan says, stop interrupting him."

JJ scoffed. "I'm not a camper. I'm practically a camp counselor. I'm here to help my yeye." Billy remembered that *yeye* meant "grandfather" in Chinese. JJ pointed over everyone's heads. "*That's* the twelfth camper." He rolled his eyes. "Apparently my yeye sees something special in her, too. Although who knows what."

Everyone turned to see a Chinese girl with a round face and two long black braids hurrying toward them.

"I'm sorry I'm late!" she said, going to stand next to Old Gold. "I was taking a nap and slept through my alarm. I was having the most delicious dream."

Old Gold sighed, rather heavily. "Everyone, this is Ling-Fei. And as JJ says, she is our twelfth camper."

Ling-Fei grinned widely at everyone and waved.

"Now, where was I?" muttered Old Gold. "Ah, yes. It is my privilege to welcome you all here. I know from your nominations that you are all looking to improve your language skills, but here you will achieve more than that. You will discover yourselves. I challenge you to open your minds and your hearts. You will only get out of this special place what you put in."

"A bit of a tall order for a summer camp," said Dylan under his breath, nudging Billy in the ribs. Billy swallowed a laugh. Despite Dylan being unlike any of his friends at home, he was starting to think maybe he wasn't too bad. Even if he wasn't a surfer and everything seemed to make him anxious.

Old Gold untied his necklace and plucked a bead from one of the ends. He held it in front of him between his finger and thumb. "This is your first assignment," he said. He took the bead and tossed it directly at Charlotte, who caught it right away. The bead gave off a light purple shimmer and was about the size of an acorn. Old Gold smiled as he pulled another bead from his necklace and tossed it to Dylan, who fumbled it between two open hands before letting it fall to the ground.

"Does this mean I fail the first assignment?" asked Dylan, looking morose.

Old Gold let out a deep laugh. "No need to worry, Dylan. A little dirt won't hurt." Old Gold continued to pull beads from his necklace and toss them around until everyone was holding one. "Each of your journeys here at Camp Dragon will be a personal one," he said. "I want you to close your eyes, open your minds and your hearts, and think about what you want most from your time here."

Billy held the bead in his hand and closed his eyes, feeling a bit silly. He opened them again and saw that everyone else's eyes were shut, their expressions earnest. He sighed and closed his eyes again. He was here now. He might as well try. He rolled the bead in his palm and thought about how far he was from home. How different everything felt here. Nothing was familiar. Even the air smelled different from the salt-scented ocean breeze he was used to. As the wind rustled his hair, he listened to the insects and birds chirping around him, the distant rushing water, and the occasional howl of the monkeys. He thought about how far from home he was, and it gave him a pang in his chest.

Focus, he told himself. What did he want from his time at camp?

On the journey here, Billy's only thought had been how much he was dreading the summer at this camp and all of the things he would miss at home. And now as he stood, listening to the new sounds and breathing in the mountain air, a tiny trickle of excitement crept in. If he *had* to be here, he might as well have a bit of an adventure. This felt like the kind of place for that.

The bead sparked unexpectedly in his hand and his eyes flew open. Old Gold was staring straight at him. Billy shut his eyes quickly, feeling like he'd been caught doing something he shouldn't. Billy shook his head, trying to refocus, but before he could gather his thoughts, Old Gold clapped. "Very good, very good. I hope that helped center everyone." He walked around and collected the beads, stringing them back onto his necklace. For a moment Billy thought his bead was glimmering. And were some of the other beads too? He blinked. Perhaps it was just a trick of the light.

"Now, what would you think if I told you that these beads are going to help me divide you into groups for the summer?" asked Old Gold with a grin.

"I'd say that you are absolutely off your rocker," Dylan said cheerfully.

Old Gold laughed. "I like your honesty," he said. "Even so, that is what I'm going to do. You might have noticed I'm just a bit old—" he paused and winked, as if letting them in on a secret "—and in my years I've learned that some things can't be explained, but that doesn't mean you shouldn't let them guide you."

Old Gold ran the necklace through his fingers and closed his eyes, humming to himself and rocking back and forth.

"This does not seem like a legitimate way to group us at all," said Charlotte, crossing her arms. "Surely we should be divided into groups based on our skills?"

Billy couldn't help agreeing. Now not only was he stuck on a mountain in the middle of China with no cell phone service, he was also at a camp run by an old man who believed in magic beads.

"Billy Chan!" Old Gold thundered, and Billy jumped.

"Dylan O'Donnell!"

"Charlotte Bell!"

"Liu Ling-Fei!"

Old Gold opened his eyes. "The beads tell me you four belong together," he said. "And who am I to disagree?"

Old Gold divided the remaining eight campers into two more groups and beamed at everyone. "I think we are off to a very good start, don't you?" The campers eyed each other warily.

"Now," Old Gold continued, "I'm sure you'd all like to get to know each other, and you can do that over lunch. But first, I want to introduce you to the other camp counselors." He gestured to three adults standing on the edge of the group, two women and a man. "This is Lee laoshi, Feng laoshi, and Wu laoshi," he said, putting the Chinese word for "teacher" after their surnames. The other camp counselors waved. "If you have any questions, or need anything at all, you can find us in the main cabins in the center of camp. Now off you go to the canteen!"

"Well," said Charlotte when they reached the canteen, "we should probably sit together, shouldn't we? If we're going to be part of a team. I'll admit all my pageant training has made me fiercely competitive; I'm going to want to win all of the activities we do."

"It isn't about winning," said Ling-Fei earnestly. "It's about the experience."

"That is what people say who don't usually win," said Charlotte. "Now that you're on my team, Ling-Fei, you can get used to winning." She winked and flounced off to get her tray.

The food was plentiful and delicious. Billy devoured mountains of fried rice and all the dumplings he could eat. So far, the food was the best part of Camp Dragon. He still wasn't sure what to think about the other campers, especially his new teammates. He liked Dylan all right, and Ling-Fei seemed nice enough, if a little strange. And he figured he'd rather have Charlotte on his team than be competing against her. He didn't doubt her commitment to winning.

"I'm so pleased we're all on the same team," said Ling-Fei with a shy smile at the group. "Now that we've met, I can feel that we are going to be friends, can't you?"

Her heartfelt enthusiasm made Billy feel awkward. He rubbed the back of his neck. "Sure," he said. Maybe the easiest way to get through the next ten weeks at camp was to just go with the flow. He was good at that. The brief spark of excitement he'd felt when he'd been holding the bead upon arrival had sputtered out, leaving him feeling resigned. He wondered what his friends at home were doing right now.

"Don't you ever feel like you've been waiting your whole life to meet the right people, for something to happen? And then when it does . . . _BAM_!" Ling-Fei threw her hands up in the air for extra emphasis, startling Dylan, who dropped his chopsticks.

Ling-Fei laughed, the sound tinkling like bells in the air. "This feels like that," she said. "Can't you feel it?"

"I think all I'm feeling is a bit of jet lag," Billy said

with a yawn. "I'm going to go find my cabin. And maybe take a nap."

If Ling-Fei was disappointed by Billy's lack of enthusiasm, she didn't show it. Instead she nodded. "Good idea! Let's all go and find our cabins."

It turned out that Billy and Dylan were sharing a cabin, and Ling-Fei and Charlotte had the one next to them. The other campers were sharing cabins with their groups, too. Billy was glad that he was sharing a cabin with someone he'd already met.

"I'm going to go find some wild flowers to decorate our cabin," Charlotte announced. "Interior decorating is one of my talents. Come on, Ling-Fei, you can show me where to find some."

Billy was pretty sure he'd never met anyone with so much confidence or so many self-professed talents as Charlotte. She seemed like the kind of person who constantly demanded attention, and right at this moment, Billy found her kind of draining. He was relieved to see her and Ling-Fei head out of the cabin and into the woods.

But it wasn't just Charlotte. It was *everything*. Being at camp, meeting new people, hoping that everyone liked him. Billy wished he were back in California. Even though he would have never have admitted it to them, he missed his parents. And his know-it-all older brother, Eddie. He wondered what they would make of all this.

He knew what they would tell him, though. His mom would tell him he was lucky to have such a great opportunity. His dad would tell him that he'd be happy he'd done this when he was older. And Eddie . . . well,

Eddie would ruffle his hair (he knew Billy was vain about his hair) and tell him to suck it up, but then he'd say that he was proud of him for being brave enough to go so far from home.

With the thoughts of his family comforting him, Billy went to check out his cabin with Dylan. It was remarkably plain, with two beds, two desks, and two dressers. That was all. There was a communal bathroom that everyone at camp shared. Billy had never shared a bathroom with anyone but his family, and he wasn't looking forward to it.

"Billy," said Dylan as they unpacked their bags, "I should probably tell you I snore."

Billy sighed. It was going to be a long summer.

CHAPTER 4
A SKY FULL OF STARS

That night, Old Gold gathered everyone around the firepit. Overhead, the stars came out—first one, then another, and then so many all at once that Billy lost count. He'd never seen so many stars in his whole life.

He'd taken a nap after lunch and was feeling slightly more energized about everything. Now, under a sky full of stars, the small part of him that yearned for adventure this summer sparked to life again, bigger than before.

"Did you guys see that shooting star?" said Kwaku, the boy from Ghana, pointing above them.

"Look! Another one!" said Charlotte.

They all watched the shooting stars for a few moments, and Billy made a wish.

He wished that he could do something at camp to make his parents and Eddie proud. What exactly, he didn't know, but Eddie had always been the one his parents were proud of, and even though that was annoying, Billy looked up to him. Maybe, just once, *he* could be the one they bragged about.

He looked around the firepit at all the new faces. Dylan, his eyes wide open and twinkling with humor, Charlotte, currently explaining the workings of shooting stars to a bewildered-looking boy next to her, and Ling-Fei, her face eager and shining in the firelight. Yes, he'd try to make the most of this summer. And maybe, just maybe, he'd make a few friends along the way.

"Are there shooting stars every night?" asked a girl with light brown skin and short dark hair. It took Billy a second to remember her name. Shreya, from Mumbai.

Old Gold smiled. "Yes. We're lucky up here in the mountains. Most nights are clear enough to see the stars. Unless there is a storm, and then the clouds are so low you can almost touch them." He pointed above them. "Do you all see that bright star there, the one right above us?"

Billy squinted up at the sky. He found it impossible to differentiate among so many stars. They were brighter than he'd ever seen at home.

The kids all shifted and tilted their heads, trying to find the star that Old Gold was pointing at.

"Oh!" said Shreya. "*That* one!" Billy followed her line of sight and his eyes widened. It was true, one was shining especially bright. Once he'd seen it, it was impossible not to notice.

"That is the Dragon's Heart," said Old Gold.

"I've never heard of that one," said Dylan, with a slight frown. "Is it like the North Star?"

Old Gold shook his head with a grin. "Not exactly. Everyone knows the North Star. But this star . . . this star is special to this mountain. We are in the perfect place to see it. I'm sure that other men have seen it—"

"And women," Charlotte interrupted.

Old Gold smiled again. "Yes, Charlotte. I'm sure others have seen it, but I am sure they have different names for it. This is a name that has been passed down in my family for generations. We believe it is called the Dragon's Heart because of a great battle that happened right here, on this very mountain, many years ago."

"Who was battling?" asked Billy, his interest bubbling out of him as he looked away from the sky and toward Old Gold through the flickering orange flames.

"It was a battle between legends. A battle between dragons," said Old Gold, a bit breathless with excitement. In the shifting shadows of the firelight, Billy thought Old Gold looked like an ancient sorcerer about to cast a spell. And Billy found himself leaning forward, eager to hear more about the battle. About the dragons.

"I thought it was a real battle," someone said, sounding a little disappointed.

"And it was!" said Old Gold, affronted. "Why do you think this mountain is called Dragon Mountain? This used to be where dragons roamed. Only the truly worthy could walk beside them. Legend says that sometimes the dragons bestowed their powers on the humans that they bonded with."

"What kind of powers?" asked Billy. He was curious despite himself. It had been years since he'd believed in things like dragons or any kind of magic at all, but sometimes, when he was surfing, he'd imagine he was riding not a wave but a mythical beast. And, he had to admit, sitting around a roaring fire in the shadow of the towering mountain with stars shooting overhead and a yearning for adventure fluttering in his heart, this felt like a place where dragons might really have existed.

Old Gold's eyes widened. "Too many powers to name! Dragons are like sorcerers. They have all kinds of magic." He said this as if it were a fact, like tigers having stripes.

"Well, what happened to them?" said Dylan, leaning closer to the fire.

"For a long time, they lived in peace alongside the humans they befriended. But then one dragon became more powerful than all the rest. The other dragons didn't like that. And so they fought. The battle was so fierce and brutal that a river of dragon blood ran from the mountain itself."

In the smoke from the fire, Billy could have sworn he saw the shape of dragons emerge. He could practically hear their roars in the crackling of the flames.

"I don't believe that a river of blood ran from the mountain," said Dylan flatly.

"Dylan," said Charlotte, throwing a stone at him. "Stop ruining the story."

"I'm just saying," said Dylan. "A river of dragon blood sounds a little far-fetched." He paused. "What happened next?"

"Oh, not if you aren't interested," said Old Gold. He gave an exaggerated yawn. "I'm getting tired myself."

"Tell us the rest of the story, Yeye," said Ling-Fei.

Old Gold wasn't really her grandfather, but she'd told them earlier he'd been good friends with her grandparents, and she'd always called him that.

"Does anyone else want to hear the rest?" said Old Gold, glancing around. "I don't want to bore you on your first night."

Around the circle there were nods and cries of "Yes, keep going!"

"Very well," said Old Gold, settling back against the tree he was leaning on. "The river of dragon blood ran, and still the battle raged. Even the stars couldn't help but watch. And then, when the battle was finally done, as even the worst battles must come to an end, the stars were so impressed with what they had seen, they took the heart of one of the slain and put it in the sky—as a reminder to all other dragons, and humans, too, of how even the mighty can fall."

"What happened after that?" said Dylan. "That doesn't sound like the end of the story. Who won?"

"That is not for us humans to know. But after this battle, dragons were never seen here again. Perhaps they battled until all were dead. Perhaps they joined the stars in the sky. Or perhaps . . ." Old Gold paused.

"Perhaps what?" asked Billy, unable to contain himself. All this talk about dragons had brought back a memory from when he was little—he and Eddie would go to the hill behind their house and lie in the grass for hours, staring up at the sky, hoping for a glimpse of a dragon.

They hadn't done that in a long time.

"Perhaps the dragons are just biding their time, waiting for the right moment to return," said Old Gold. He yawned, a real yawn this time. "I can't stay awake another minute. I'm heading to bed, and—" he looked at all of them with his sternest expression, which really wasn't that stern at all "—I expect all of you to do the same within the next five minutes."

"Yes, Old Gold," they chorused.

"Good night," said Old Gold, and with a groan he pulled himself to his feet and walked back toward his cabin.

Later, Billy lay in bed, staring up at the unfamiliar ceiling.

"Dylan?" he whispered, but the only reply was Dylan's deep breathing and an occasional snore. He hadn't been kidding about that.

Billy had thought he'd fall asleep right away, but his mind was buzzing. He'd enjoyed tonight. More than he'd expected. And the story Old Gold had told about the dragons swam around in his brain, making him remember how much he really did love legends and magic.

He realized that if he had stayed home this summer, he knew exactly what he would be doing. Knew exactly what his summer would look like. There was comfort in that, but it wasn't very exciting.

Here, he didn't know what to expect. And to Billy's surprise, he found he quite liked that idea.

CHAPTER 5
THE STORM

Billy woke to the light pitter-patter of rainfall on the roof of their cabin and Dylan snoring.

He rolled over in his bed and looked out of the window.

The camp had turned into a mud pit overnight. Through the rain-fogged windowpane, he could see other campers making their way to the canteen, presumably for breakfast.

"Dylan," he said. "Dylan, wake up."

Dylan grunted and buried himself deeper into his bed.

Billy threw a pillow at him. "Come on, it's time for breakfast."

"It sounds like it's *raining*," Dylan muttered. "I don't want to go out in the rain. I get enough of that at home in Ireland."

"So you'd rather stay in here and starve?"

Dylan moaned and rolled over. "Fine, fine. If th are my *only* options, I guess I'll take a little rain."

In the canteen, the other campers huddled around the breakfast tables, with wet hair and muddy shoes. Nobody looked happy. Billy wondered if it was an ominous start to the summer. Any hope he'd had about exploring the campgrounds had been washed away by the rain; he had a feeling they were going to be stuck inside all day, damp and smelly and bored.

"Why does everyone look so glum?" asked Charlotte, dipping a piece of fried dough into her bowl of congee. Dylan kept calling the congee "rice porridge," which it kind of was. "It's just a little rain," she added.

"I like this weather," said Ling-Fei, looking out at the rain pounding on the windows of the canteen. "I wish we could go and run and dance in the rain, but Old Gold will want us to stay indoors."

"I'm with Old Gold on this one," said Dylan, taking a sip of his hot chocolate. "I personally do *not* want to catch a cold. But you are welcome to go gallivanting in the rain if that sounds like your idea of fun."

"I don't mind the rain either," said Billy. "At home, I surf every morning, even in the rain. But it is one thing to be in the ocean in the rain when you're already wet—it's a swamp out there. No thank you."

"If you all love the rain so much, you really should come visit me in Ireland one day," said Dylan, slurping up more hot chocolate.

Old Gold hurried into the canteen, wearing a giant rain hat and raincoat that went all the way to the floor. Only his beard stuck out.

"Good morning, campers!" Old Gold said. "Due to the inclement weather, we're going to have to postpone our scheduled activity. Instead, today you'll have your first Mandarin lesson, followed by a cooking class with Wu laoshi in the kitchens and then a kung fu demonstration with Lee laoshi." He clapped his hands. "Now, off you go!"

In their Mandarin lesson, Billy was surprised at how well Dylan spoke Chinese.

"Dude," he said in admiration, "you're really good. How long have you been studying Chinese?"

Dylan shrugged. "I've always liked languages," he said. "So I started teaching myself Chinese a few years ago." He flushed. "I know, I know, I'm a nerd. But that's why I was so excited when the librarian at my school told me she'd put me forward for this summer camp. You probably think that's really lame, right?" The tips of his ears turned red.

Billy shook his head and grinned at Dylan. "No, it's actually kind of cool."

Dylan beamed.

Later, Wu laoshi, a short, round man with a big head, showed them how to make mapo tofu, a spicy stew of tofu and minced pork. Billy loved mapo tofu. It was one of his favorite dishes that his dad made, and the mouth-numbing spice from the dish reminded him of home. Dylan took one bite, and his eyes started streaming. "This is . . . spicy," he said.

"I can handle it," said Charlotte. "I'd like it even spicier! I put hot sauce on everything at home. I've got a very high tolerance for spice. And an excellent palate overall."

"Of course you do," said Billy under his breath.

During Lee laoshi's kung fu demonstration, Billy expected to feel silly as they practiced the basic moves, but he found he was a bit of a natural. Meanwhile, Charlotte was getting confused with her jujitsu moves, and Dylan's glasses kept falling off. "It's only the first day," said Lee laoshi, "Just wait till the end of camp. You'll all be kung fu pros."

At the end of the day, it was still raining, and even walking from the cabin to the bathroom to get ready for bed felt like a trek. Billy was exhausted, but in a satisfying way, like when he came home after a long day of surfing. Even though they had been indoors the whole time, he'd had fun. Especially in the cooking and kung fu classes. Still, he hoped that it would stop raining by tomorrow so he could explore more of the campgrounds.

"I do *not* want to go back out in that," said Dylan when he and Billy were back in their cabin. He sat on his bed and wrapped his blanket tight around him.

"I'm sure the weather will be better in the morning," said Billy with a yawn as he climbed into his bed. He found the sound of the rain on the roof soothing, and soon he drifted off to sleep.

Billy didn't know how long he'd been asleep when a crash of thunder woke him. He jolted up and looked over at Dylan, who was sound asleep and snoring loud enough to be heard over the rain.

Billy settled back into bed and closed his eyes. After a few moments, he opened them, squirming with a very uncomfortable realization.

He had to pee.

He waited for as long as he could and then got up and put on his jacket.

As soon as he stepped outside the door, he was pelted with raindrops from all directions. He put his head down and hurried toward the bathrooms.

On his way back to his cabin, lightning flashed above him, setting the sky alight. Thunder followed, so loud and so close that Billy could have sworn he felt the ground shake. Blinking, he stepped under the awning of the nearest cabin for shelter as his eyes adjusted.

He blinked again, trying to clear his vision. Had he just seen a flash of lightning *inside* the cabin? There! Again! A flash of blue light, zigzagging across the cabin, illuminating it from the inside. And in the center of the room, emitting its own light, sat a glowing silver orb. The blue lightning seemed to be coming from it or going toward it, Billy wasn't sure. But he *was* sure he was seeing something very strange.

A crash of thunder snapped Billy back to his senses, and he was suddenly very aware of his soggy feet and wet hair. With a final glance back at the strange blue light, he ran to his own cabin, wondering what he'd just seen.

CHAPTER 6
THE GREAT RACE

The next morning dawned bright and clear. Water droplets glistened from the cabin eaves and tree branches. Billy rubbed his eyes, remembering what he'd seen last night. Or at least what he'd *thought* he'd seen. A mysterious glowing blue orb. Now, in the bright morning sun, it seemed ridiculous. It had been late, he'd been tired, and it had probably been the reflection of the lightning on the window. He put it out of his mind and hurried to the canteen for breakfast.

Everyone was in much better spirits today. There was a giddy buzz of excitement in the air. After breakfast, Old Gold called the campers to the tree stump in the clearing.

"Now that the weather has decided to cooperate, we can have our first official camp challenge!" He unfurled a scroll showing twelve animals, with a rat at the top and a pig at the bottom. "Does anyone know what these animals are?"

This, Billy knew. He put his hand up quickly, even faster than Charlotte. "The animals in the Chinese zodiac," he said.

Old Gold beamed. "Correct! What you might *not* know is that a very, very, *very* long time ago there was a Great Race to determine which twelve animals would make it into the zodiac and what their order would be." He paused and chuckled. "As you can see, the rat won the race and came in first. But what you won't see is a cat in the zodiac. That's because the cat and rat worked together to get to the front, but then the rat pushed the cat into the river, which is why to this day cats hate water and will always try to catch rats." He rolled up the scroll. "Now, I thought it would be fun to have our own Great Race to determine which group can work the best together."

Old Gold hopped off the tree stump and handed each group a single red envelope. "In each of these envelopes is a riddle that describes an object found in this region of China. Your challenge is to solve the riddle and bring me that object. Remember, it isn't just about speed. The rat won the race through cunning. I'm not saying to follow the rat's example and push the other team into a river"— he chuckled again—"but you will need to use your brains, too! The order you finish in will determine the order in which you get to choose things for the rest of your team here at camp, from meals to special excursions."

He looked over at Billy and his team. "Now, I realize Ling-Fei's team is at a bit of an advantage as she is more familiar with the area, so you have been given a more difficult riddle with something harder to find."

"That doesn't seem fair," Charlotte muttered. Billy agreed but didn't say anything. He liked Ling-Fei fine, but right at this moment it felt like having her on their team was more of a disadvantage if it meant they were being given a harder challenge. Even if he wasn't as outwardly competitive as Charlotte, he wanted to win, too.

"The first team back in this very spot wins. Let the race begin!" shouted Old Gold. He threw a small ball high into the air, and it exploded into a cloud of red and gold confetti. "GO!"

Charlotte snatched the envelope from Dylan and ripped it open. "We've got to win this," she said.

"Someone is a bit competitive, aren't they?" said Dylan.

"Stay focused and pay attention," said Charlotte as she pulled a small gold card from the envelope and read it aloud:

"I bear the name of an almighty beast, but beneath my spikes and scales, I am a treat to eat."

"Any ideas?" Dylan asked after a short pause.

Billy sighed. He was terrible at solving riddles. The last time he'd gotten the right answer for a riddle was only because he'd seen the answer sheet beforehand. "Maybe it's some sort of animal?"

"It's *obviously* an animal," huffed Charlotte. "Spikes? Scales? What *else* could it be?"

Billy crossed his arms. "You know, for someone who wants to win so badly, you aren't making it very easy for us."

"If we're going to finish first, we need to work together," Ling-Fei said, stepping in between them. She took Billy and Charlotte's hands in each of hers as she closed her eyes. "Close your eyes and take a deep breath with me."

Billy and Charlotte watched as Ling-Fei closed her eyes and took a long breath. Billy knew what she was trying to do, but instead of helping him become less annoyed at Charlotte, now he was annoyed at Ling-Fei, too.

"Don't you feel so much more relaxed?" Ling-Fei opened her eyes to find Billy and Charlotte still staring at her.

"We're wasting time!" said Charlotte. "The other teams are already going off to find their item!"

"You were both supposed to be taking a deep breath with me!" said Ling-Fei, her voice faltering a bit.

"And you're supposed to be the local expert!" snapped Charlotte.

"Whoa, whoa, whoa," said Dylan. "We're all on the same team, with the same goal. So here is what we know based on the clues." He held out an open hand and started counting his fingers. "We know that it is something with spikes and scales, something that we can eat, and something that is named after a beast." Dylan paused and pushed his glasses back up on his face.

"Thank you for just rephrasing the riddle," said Charlotte, rolling her eyes.

"Only trying to help," said Dylan, forcing a smile.

An awkward tension filled the air.

Charlotte closed her eyes and took in a long breath. She paused a moment before opening her eyes. "You're right. You're all right, I'm sorry." She looked at Ling-Fei and offered a tentative smile. "The deep breath helped."

Ling-Fei gave her a small smile back.

"Scales, scales . . . maybe it's a fish?" Charlotte went on.

"Good thinking!" said Dylan "But what kind of fish has spikes and is also named after a beast?"

A thought dawned on Billy. Last summer he discovered the strangest fish he'd ever seen. He'd remembered it because it was called a lionfish, although in his opinion it didn't look anything like a lion—because it was covered in spikes! "I've got it!" he said. "It's a lionfish! It's named after a beast, it has spikes and scales, and I'm pretty sure you can eat it."

"Good thinking, Billy!" said Charlotte. "That must be it!" She turned to Ling-Fei. "Where around here can we find a lionfish?"

"Aren't lionfish *extremely* dangerous? I'm pretty sure they can kill you," said Dylan.

"What else could it be?" said Billy.

Ling-Fei's face lit up. "I know what it is! It's a *dragon*!" She started to laugh. "Old Gold must think he is so clever."

"You can't eat mythical creatures," said Billy, who still wanted his answer to be right.

"It's dragon *fruit*!" Ling-Fei replied with a smile. "It fits the description perfectly—they have spikes and scales, or at least what look like scales, and they are delicious! And best of all, I know just where we can find one."

Ling-Fei led the group into the forest. As he followed her, Billy noticed she was chewing her lower lip anxiously.

"What's wrong?" he asked.

Ling-Fei looked around nervously. "You know how Old Gold said he gave us a more difficult item to find?"

Billy nodded.

"He wasn't kidding. The place I know where dragon fruit grows is far. But . . ." She trailed off.

"But what?" prompted Billy.

"I know a shortcut. I'm not supposed to know about it—it's through the bamboo grove, which is technically off limits . . ."

"You know a shortcut?" asked Charlotte, who had snuck up next to them. "Well, we absolutely must use that. You heard Old Gold: the rat won by cunning."

"I don't know," said Ling-Fei. "I don't want us to get in trouble."

"How will Old Gold even know we took a shortcut?" Charlotte said. She looked at Billy and Dylan. "You two agree with me, right?"

"She's got a point," said Dylan.

"I do kind of want to win," Billy admitted.

"Okay," said Ling-Fei hesitantly. "It's this way."

They walked deeper into the forest until they reached a lake edged with weeping willows and then, beyond that, a bamboo grove. It felt like stepping into a painting.

Billy stopped. There was something moving in the bamboo up ahead.

"Did you guys see that?" he asked, pointing. "There's something there."

"It's probably a monkey," said Ling-Fei. "I'm sure we'll see a few. They're mostly harmless. They've taken over that pavilion up ahead. That's why it's called Monkey Pavilion. The dragon fruit plants are just on the other side."

"Did you say the monkeys are *mostly* harmless?" Dylan squawked, but the rest of the group was already heading toward the bamboo.

As they passed the weeping willows and stepped into the bamboo, the air and light around them changed. Sunlight filtered down in strips, and when Billy tilted his head back, he could only see pockets of sky. He hadn't realized how tall the bamboo grew.

"Shouldn't we hear the monkeys?" asked Charlotte. "It's awfully quiet."

"Maybe they know we're coming and are waiting to ambush us," said Dylan.

Billy laughed and swatted Dylan on the back. "Relax," he said. "We're bigger than them."

"And *some* of us are smarter than them, too," quipped Charlotte.

Soon, the bamboo opened into a small glade. In the center stood a red pavilion with a sloping green roof supported by four pillars. The edges of the roof were upturned and the top was pointed.

And there was something on the pavilion, staring straight at them.

"Guys," Dylan breathed, "that's not a monkey."

CHAPTER 7
DON'T RUN

Billy stopped breathing. Staring straight at them was a tiger. Its long orange fur was striped with black, and its eyes were a vivid yellow. Even from a distance, Billy could see its claws glinting in the light.

"This isn't happening, this isn't happening," Dylan whispered, his eyes tightly shut.

"What do we do?" Billy asked. He felt frozen to the spot, like he was in a dream where he couldn't move. He tried to remember if he knew anything about tigers. But all he could focus on was the one directly in front of them.

"I don't know," Ling-Fei whispered back, her eyes huge.

"We shouldn't run," Charlotte said. "I know that much from watching animal documentaries."

"Do you think it has seen us?" Dylan said, his eyes still closed. "Maybe it doesn't know we're here."

As if in response, the tiger licked its lips, its pink tongue flicking out again and again.

"It has definitely seen us," whimpered Ling-Fei.

The tiger stood up and stretched. Its muscles rippled under its fur, and Billy knew without a doubt that it could tear him apart.

He could only think of one other time he'd been this frightened. He'd been surfing, alone, and a wave had knocked him off and under his board. He hadn't been able to tell which way was up, and he'd been certain he was going to die.

He had the same feeling now. A cold, dark feeling that spread throughout his entire body. Then, he'd kicked and struggled and swam till the ocean spat him out. Now, his heart hammering in his chest so loud he was sure the tiger could hear it, he tried to stay as still as he could. Everything around him seemed to come more into focus—the colors were brighter, he could smell the dirt of the forest floor, and he thought he could even see the tiger's whiskers quivering.

"Don't move," Ling-Fei whispered without moving her mouth.

"What's it doing?" asked Dylan, less quietly than Ling-Fei.

"Dylan, shut up and stay still," Charlotte hissed.

Dylan opened one eye and inhaled so loudly Billy had to stop himself from throwing his hand over Dylan's mouth.

"We are so dead!" Dylan said, starting to tremble.

"Dylan, stay calm," whispered Billy, taking the

smallest of steps closer to him. "Just breathe." Billy said this as much to himself as to Dylan. He knew if he focused on keeping Dylan calm, he wouldn't be able to think about how terrified *he* was.

Dylan breathed out a long, loud, shuddering breath.

"Breathe quieter," Charlotte whispered.

The tiger started making its way down the steps of the pavilion, its eyes on them. Billy felt Dylan tense and could sense he was about to take off.

"Stay still. It'll think you are prey if you run," Billy whispered as loud as he dared.

"We *are* prey!" said Dylan. But he didn't move.

Billy wondered if they should try to scare the tiger off, the way he had heard you could do with a bear. Maybe they should get together and try to make themselves as big as possible. He didn't have time to make that decision, though.

By now the tiger was so close that Billy could have taken two steps forward and touched its pink nose. Then, right as the tiger almost reached them, it veered left, its thick tail swaying as it circled behind them.

"Wh-what's it d-doing?" Dylan stammered.

"I think it's going away," said Ling-Fei.

None of them dared to look over their shoulders, but Billy could feel the tiger's yellow eyes boring into their backs.

There was a rustle, followed by a low growl.

"It's going to eat us!" Dylan shouted, and he sprinted toward the pavilion.

"Dylan! Wait!" called Ling-Fei.

With a mighty roar, the tiger leaped over Billy, Ling-Fei, and Charlotte and chased after Dylan into the trees beyond.

The other three looked at each other in a panic. "We have to go after him," said Billy. "Come on!"

He ran as fast as he could without really knowing what he was going to do once he caught up. He just knew he couldn't abandon Dylan.

He could see flashes of orange ahead, and just a bit farther, the back of Dylan's head.

"Do you have a plan?" shouted Charlotte, catching up to Billy as he dodged a low-hanging branch.

"I was hoping one of you did," Billy shouted back.

"With four of us together, we might be able to hold the tiger off!" said Ling-Fei, coming up on his other side.

They raced through the trees, monkeys howling and shouting in the branches above, and burst into another clearing. They found Dylan backed against a sheer limestone wall, holding his hands over his face.

There was no sign of the tiger.

"Dylan! Come on, let's get out of here!" yelled Billy, running toward him.

Dylan looked up in a panic. "Stop!" he cried. "The tiger is right there!"

But it was too late. When Billy turned toward where Dylan was pointing, he saw the tiger standing above them on a massive boulder. It stared at them for a long moment, before letting out a fierce roar.

Instinctively, the four moved closer together. Billy reached out to grab Charlotte's hand on his right and

Dylan's on his left just as Ling-Fei took Dylan's other hand.

As they stood there, linked, Billy felt like time had stopped. A jolt ran through their intertwined hands. It was like the same strange adrenaline rush he felt when he took a huge wave while surfing.

The tiger jumped off the boulder, landing a few paces away from them. There was nowhere for them to go. No way for them to stop whatever happened next.

It was odd then, Billy thought, that he didn't feel as afraid anymore. His earlier sense of dread and fear had gone. Instead, he felt a kind of calm strength. Like he could face anything. Even a tiger. He gripped his friends' hands tighter.

And then the strangest thing happened.

The tiger seemed to inhale deeply, its whiskers twitching. It took a few steps back and let out another roar.

"Do you think it's calling for its friends?" Dylan whispered.

The tiger looked at them again with its piercing yellow eyes, and with a roar, it leaped into the air straight at them. Someone, maybe Charlotte, screamed.

Billy shut his eyes, waiting for the worst . . .

CHAPTER 8
KNOCKED OFF COURSE

"DID YOU SEE THAT?" Dylan shouted.

Billy's eyes flew open.

The tiger was gone.

Billy blinked. "My eyes were closed," he admitted. "What happened?"

"It's gone," breathed Ling-Fei. "It's really gone."

"I mean, it just disappeared *into* the mountain!" said Dylan. He looked over his shoulder. "Where could it have gone?"

"I don't care *where* it has gone, as long as it *has* gone," said Charlotte, sagging against the rock. Billy and the others followed suit. They were still holding hands, he realized, even though there was no real reason to now. In a funny way Billy felt like his grip on Charlotte and Dylan was his grip on reality. If he let go, would he disappear the way the tiger had?

"There has to be a rational explanation," said Dylan. "Tigers don't just disappear." He cleared his throat. "Also. Thank you. For coming after me." He paused. "Although if I had known it was just going to disappear, I wouldn't have run off, but who could have known *that*?"

"Yeah, well, next time maybe don't run when we tell you to stay still," said Ling-Fei with a smile.

"I sincerely hope there will never be a next time. I have no desire to encounter a tiger, or any other wild animal, ever again," Dylan said.

An unexpected laugh escaped Billy, and soon the others were laughing, too. Big belly laughs tinged with relief.

They were still laughing when the ground began to shake.

At first Billy thought it was their laughter making them shake. Then he heard the crack behind them.

"You guys . . ." he said, stepping away from the mountain. Billy knew from growing up in California that when an earthquake struck, you didn't want to be anywhere near something that could fall on you.

Rocks started tumbling down the mountain, and one landed directly where the tiger had been.

"It's an earthquake!" shouted Billy, pulling the others away. "Let's get out of here!" He knew they had to find somewhere to wait out the tremors.

There was another loud crack and, to Billy's horror, he saw a cleft open in the mountain face. "We have to get away!" he cried. "Back to the clearing!"

They tried to run through the forest, but the ground

was rolling beneath them. It threw them with every step they took.

"Slow down!" cried Ling-Fei.

"I'm worried about the trees!" Billy gestured above them. "I don't want one to fall on us."

"THERE!" yelled Charlotte, pointing ahead of them. "There's the clearing."

In between tremors, they made it to the clearing and collapsed as the ground continued to rumble beneath them.

Billy lost all sense of time.

Finally, the shaking subsided. Billy wasn't sure if the earthquake had lasted minutes or hours.

The four lay still for a few minutes, not speaking, just breathing heavily.

The ground had stopped shaking, but Billy's hands still trembled. He'd been in earthquakes before, but never anything like this. It had felt like the ground was going to open up and swallow them. He thought maybe it still might. Or that the mountain behind them would crash down on them at any moment. He felt far from home, far from anything familiar or safe.

He glanced over at Charlotte, Dylan, and Ling-Fei, all still staring up at the sky in a dazed way. At least they were together.

"Well," said Charlotte, sitting up and dusting some dirt off her dress. "We are having quite a day, aren't we?"

Billy snorted. "That's one way of putting it." He felt surprisingly reassured by how unbothered Charlotte seemed to be. Maybe she hadn't realized how much danger they had really been in. Maybe she was far more fearless than Billy. Or maybe she was putting on a brave face. Whatever it was, he was glad she was there.

Dylan rolled over. "I'm alive! We're all alive!"

"I've been in earthquakes in California, but I've never felt one like that before," said Billy. His hands had stopped trembling, but he still felt shaken. "I've never seen the ground jump like that."

"We should get back to camp," said Ling-Fei. "I want to make sure Old Gold is okay!"

"But do you think it's safe for us to head back?" asked Dylan. He turned to Billy. "You are our resident earthquake expert. What do you think?"

"I'm definitely not an expert, but I do know there are usually aftershocks."

"We don't know for sure it was an earthquake," said Ling-Fei. "It might have been a landslide."

"What do you mean, we aren't sure?" sputtered Dylan. "Didn't you see the actual ground moving?"

Ling-Fei rubbed her eyes. "Yes, but I also saw a tiger disappear."

"Either way, I agree with Ling-Fei," said Billy. "We should get back to camp."

"But we don't have the dragon fruit!" said Charlotte. "We can't go back empty-handed!"

Billy raised his eyebrows in disbelief. "Forget the dragon fruit; we're lucky we're all going back in one piece." It had been a strange and terrifying morning, but they'd survived. Together.

Charlotte sighed. "Fine. Hopefully we won't be the only ones the earthquake knocked off course." She paused and looked at them expectantly. "Get it? Knocked off course? Because it almost knocked us over?"

"Too soon, Charlotte, too soon," said Dylan.

CHAPTER 9
A RATIONAL EXPLANATION

Billy was expecting pandemonium when they got back to camp. But everything seemed . . . *normal.*

Not only were all the cabins still standing, but all the other groups were back, waiting expectantly around the tree stump. Expectantly. Not worriedly. Relaxed, and not at all like they might just have narrowly escaped being crushed by a falling boulder or tree.

No, all the others had returned, completely unharmed, and each group had its respective item.

Charlotte pulled up short when she saw that they were the only group to have failed the challenge.

"This is my worst nightmare," she said, the blood draining from her face. "I can't go out there. I *never* lose."

"We were just chased by a tiger and survived an earthquake, and *this* is your worst nightmare?" asked Dylan.

"We're alive. And if I'm not dead, I'm coming in first," said Charlotte. "The earthquake apparently didn't slow down the others at all. We're the only ones who let it impact us. I've never been so embarrassed," She covered her face with her hands.

"I can think of at least twenty-three times that I've been more embarrassed," said Dylan. "*This* doesn't even come close."

"You must do very embarrassing things all the time, then," Charlotte retorted.

"I think we should just be glad that everyone else looks like they are okay," said Billy, feeling slightly wary. Something was off. How come everyone else seemed completely fine? If he hadn't been with his friends, he might have thought he'd imagined everything that'd happened in the forest.

"Is Jeremy holding a bit of bamboo? *Bamboo*? That isn't hard to find at all!" Charlotte huffed.

"I want to go let them know we are okay," said Ling-Fei. "They must be worried!"

"They don't . . . *look* very worried," said Dylan.

The four emerged from the forest, covered in dirt and with torn clothes, and empty-handed.

"Aha! Our final group has returned," said Old Gold with a wide grin. Then his forehead creased in concern. "Why are you all so dirty? Are you all right? What happened?"

"There was an earthquake," Billy said. "Didn't you feel it?"

Everyone stared at him.

"Are you losers pretending you were in an earthquake to explain why you came in last?" scoffed JJ. "Pathetic."

Ling-Fei looked at Old Gold. "We really did feel an earthquake—the trees were jumping and everything!"

Old Gold's mouth flattened into a stern line. "Ling-Fei," he said, "don't make up stories. Especially not about something so dangerous!"

"But . . ." Ling-Fei started. Old Gold hushed her with a quick shake of his head.

"That's enough," he said. "I was hoping you would be able to help your team, Ling-Fei, not hinder them."

"She was an excellent help," said Charlotte. "We solved the riddle! Dragon fruit. And we were on our way to find it through Monkey Pavilion when we saw a tiger!"

There was a pause before JJ started laughing. Loud and mean. "If you are going to lie, at least make it believable. There are no tigers in this forest."

The other kids began to giggle.

Charlotte turned red. Billy wasn't sure if it was from anger or embarrassment or both.

"And Monkey Pavilion?" said Old Gold, his frown getting deeper. "Ling-Fei, you know that is off-limits. You broke the rules and didn't even complete the task?"

"Typical Ling-Fei," sneered JJ.

Ling-Fei looked as if she were about to cry. Billy stepped forward.

"I know what we felt," he said, trying to make his voice as confident as he could, like he was someone to be taken seriously. "Something happened in that forest."

"Yeah, you got lost," said JJ, snickering.

"Billy," said Old Gold, more gently, "I am sure you are all disappointed. But if you are going to lose, lose with dignity. Lying doesn't help anyone."

Billy looked at his team and shrugged. It was obvious nobody was going to believe them.

"We're sorry, Old Gold," Dylan blurted. "We got carried away. It's my fault. I thought I saw something in the trees, and we followed it and got lost. That's what happened."

"I see," said Old Gold. "Well, I must say, I'm disappointed. Especially in you, Ling-Fei."

Ling-Fei hung her head.

"You've not only come in last, but you've ruined the celebration for the team that came in first," he said, pointing at the group with the bamboo. "Instead of celebrating their win, we are focusing on your loss."

"Well done," said Billy half-heartedly, giving the other team a thumbs-up. It felt ridiculous to be chastised for being poor sports when they were still reeling from surviving both the earthquake and the tiger. Charlotte may have been upset that they had lost, but Billy felt more frustrated that nobody believed what had happened.

"Congratulations," said Charlotte through clenched teeth. Dylan managed a smile, but he could see Ling-Fei was still too distraught to say anything.

"Now, where were we?" said Old Gold. "Ah, yes, congratulations to our winners! You have won our Great Race."

Later, the friends sat huddled around a small table in the back corner of the canteen and spoke in hushed voices.

"I don't get it. How did nobody else feel the earthquake?" said Billy, taking a bite of stir-fried noodles. The other campers kept glancing at them and whispering, and he was glad to have the other three with him. They really felt like a team now.

"I don't understand," said Dylan, shaking his head. "It is . . . well, not impossible, but highly implausible."

"And how do you explain the disappearing tiger?" said Charlotte. "And you know what? For as much as JJ is an absolute jerk, I don't think he was lying when he said there aren't tigers around here. Something weird is going on."

They ate in silence, trying to make sense of it all.

"To be honest, I wouldn't believe it if the three of you hadn't seen the same thing," said Dylan.

"Me either," said Billy. He paused and looked down at his noodles, feeling too awkward to look his new friends in the eye, considering what he was about to say. "I'm glad we were all together for it." Even though he had only met Dylan, Charlotte, and Ling-Fei the day before yesterday, after what they had been through, he felt like he'd known them much longer.

"Same," said Charlotte.

"Me, too," said Ling-Fei.

"How are you feeling, Ling-Fei?" said Billy. "Old Gold was hard on you."

Ling-Fei shrugged. "He's right to be disappointed," she said. "I shouldn't have taken you out of bounds." She raised her hand to her neck and suddenly started looking around frantically. "My necklace!" she said with a gasp.

"It's gone! It must have fallen off when we were chasing the tiger." Billy could see she was blinking back tears. "My grandmother gave it to me. It's been in my family for generations. It's my most important possession."

"Well, it's obvious, isn't it?" said Charlotte.

They all stared at her.

"What is?" said Billy.

"We have to go back," said Charlotte.

"What?" sputtered Dylan.

"We have to help Ling-Fei find her necklace," said Charlotte. "And it isn't just that." She lowered her voice. "Didn't you all feel . . . whatever that was? By the mountain?"

"I felt the *earthquake*," said Dylan. "And it made me want to stay as far away from the mountain as possible. And that tiger."

"But the tiger disappeared," said Billy. "Like it was . . ." He paused. No one had said the word out loud.

"Magic," said Charlotte. "Like it was magic."

Dylan rolled his eyes. "Oh, please. It wasn't magic! There's no such thing as magic. Just like there is no such thing as a river of dragon blood. Trust me, I'm from Ireland, the supposed home of fairies and leprechauns and all kinds of magic. I would know if magic was real."

"So how do you explain the disappearing tiger?" said Charlotte.

"Maybe it just jumped into its hidey-hole in the mountain," said Dylan. "Maybe it was a group hallucination. That can happen, you know."

"The only way to figure out what it was is to go back," said Billy.

And as he said it, he realized that he was glad they had a reason to return to the forest. Glad to go back to where something extraordinary had happened to him and his friends. Part of him was scared, but another part of him was drawn to the mystery of it. He wanted to know what had happened. Even if it had been terrifying, it had also been *exciting*.

"It's my necklace," said Ling-Fei, pushing a strand of her dark hair out of her face. "I can go on my own."

"No way," said Charlotte emphatically. "We'll find it faster if all of us look."

"She's right," said Billy. "We should stick together." He still had the feeling he'd had immediately after the earthquake, that they had survived *because* they'd been together.

Dylan sighed and put his head in his hands. "Fine," he said. He looked out the window. "But it's already getting dark. You aren't going to make me go fumbling around in the forest in the dark, are you?"

"No, we should wait till morning," said Charlotte. "Let's go first thing. Right after sunrise. That way nobody will miss us. We have free time tomorrow morning, remember? We'll just make sure we're back for class in the afternoon."

"That's really nice of you all," said Ling-Fei in a quiet voice. "I don't want to get you in trouble again."

"You heard Charlotte," said Billy. "We'll go so early nobody will even notice we've gone."

Dylan groaned and put his head in his hands. "This sounds like a terrible idea."

"Well, you don't have to come if you don't want to," said Charlotte with a huff.

Dylan looked up with a small grin. "Like I'd let you lot go off on an adventure without me."

CHAPTER 10
DISAPEARANCES

"Do you have any idea where you dropped your necklace?" asked Charlotte as they stepped into the cool shade of the forest the next morning. She sounded like a detective. Billy was surprised she didn't whip out a magnifying glass. But in this kind of situation, he appreciated her confident can-do attitude.

Ling-Fei nodded. "I still had it when we got to the pavilion because I remember rubbing it when we first saw the tiger." She paused. "I *think* I had it at the base of the mountain, too. Before the earthquake."

"The earthquake that apparently only *we* felt," said Billy, furrowing his brow.

"Right," said Charlotte brusquely. "We've got a clue, a lead, and now all we need is a plan of action. I think we should go back to the pavilion and retrace our steps to the mountain."

"What if an earthquake hits again? Or the tiger comes back?" asked Dylan.

Charlotte seemed to steel herself a little. "Then we'll deal with it."

This time, there *were* monkeys in the pavilion. Billy counted at least twelve, or he thought he did—they were moving around so fast he couldn't be sure.

"Ohhh, I hope a monkey didn't find my necklace," Ling-Fei moaned. "Then we'll never get it back." She looked up at one of the creatures. "Dear Mr. Monkey, do you have my necklace?"

"If he does, I bet he won't tell you," said Dylan.

"Let's stick to the plan and retrace our steps," Charlotte said, sounding simultaneously bossy and soothing. "There's no need to jump to any conclusions."

"I'm just glad we're dealing with monkeys and not tigers," added Dylan.

The monkeys mostly ignored them, seeming content to groom each other and hop along the roof of the pavilion to the trees overhead.

The group went around the pavilion and into the bamboo forest toward the mountain.

"What is the best way to look for the necklace?" asked Billy, rubbing the back of his neck.

"With your eyes," retorted Charlotte. "Look on the ground; it's shiny, remember? It'll stand out."

They carried on through the bamboo, keeping their eyes down. There was no sign of the necklace, but nobody said the obvious—that they might not find it.

They all knew how important it was to Ling-Fei. They kept scanning the ground and looking under bushes until they were back at the base of the mountain.

"Whoa," said Billy. Up until now, the forest had looked untouched by the earthquake. But the area around the mountain was ravaged. There were rocks and boulders everywhere, huge craters in the ground, and a long, jagged crack down the mountain face itself. At the bottom of the crack was a small triangular opening. Billy shuddered, grateful that the mountain hadn't collapsed on them.

"Hey," he said, pointing at the crack in the rock. "Do you guys see that?"

There was a thin stream of water coming out of the opening. Billy went closer. The water seemed flecked with gold.

"It's a river of gold, not a river of blood," he said almost to himself, remembering the legend Old Gold had told them. The story swirled around his brain, mixing with the memory of what had happened yesterday. Had Old Gold said anything about a tiger?

"Unless dragon blood is actually gold," said Ling-Fei, who clearly was following the same train of thought as Billy.

"You are both off your rockers," Dylan said with a sigh. "It's *clearly* a normal mountain stream that must have burst from inside the mountain after the earthquake. Basic science."

"I guess this is the proof we were looking for that the earthquake actually happened," said Charlotte, looking up the mountain.

"Should we retrace our steps?" asked Dylan, scratching his head. "Or do we think the necklace is somewhere around here?" He tentatively kicked a rock near his foot. The rock rolled over, and a beetle scuttled out from underneath it. Dylan jumped.

Billy had the peculiar feeling that someone, or something, was watching him. He looked over his shoulder at the forest, expecting to see the tiger staring at him. The hairs on the back of his neck stood up.

"You guys," he said, eyes darting around, "I think maybe we should leave."

"Billy's right," said Ling-Fei sadly. "A monkey probably found my necklace, and now it's gone forever."

"We can't give up yet," said Charlotte. "Maybe it got buried under one of these rocks," She walked to the pile of boulders next to them.

"Let me look!" said Dylan, hurrying over.

Billy couldn't shake the unsettling sensation that they weren't alone. It felt like a spider was crawling along his neck. A gust of wind swooshed by, blowing back his hair.

Dylan and Charlotte were still focused on overturning rocks.

Something was wrong. Billy was sure of it. He spun around quickly, ready to fight whatever was behind them.

There was nothing there.

Not even Ling-Fei.

CHAPTER 11
INTO THE MOUNTAIN

"Where's Ling-Fei?" said Billy, trying to push down the panic rising in his chest.

"What do you mean, where's Ling-Fei?" said Dylan, looking up. "She was right behind you." His mouth dropped open.

Charlotte hopped off the rock pile, dusting her hands off on her dress. "LING-FEI!" she shouted into the forest.

There was no answer.

Charlotte, Billy, and Dylan stared at each other. "Do you think she went looking somewhere else?" asked Dylan. "That makes sense, right? She must have just wandered off."

"We would have heard her . . . wouldn't we? She would have said something," said Billy. He turned to face the forest, trying to see if there was any movement. There was another gust of wind, but nothing else. The panic in his chest spread throughout his whole body. Billy had seen a surfer disappear beneath the waves once and not emerge when the wave had passed. This felt like that. The surfer had reappeared a few moments later in the surf, gasping for air, but there. Just like Ling-Fei was going to reappear, Billy told himself. People didn't just disappear into thin air. Billy took a deep breath. "The important thing is that we all stick together," he said, turning back to Charlotte and Dylan.

Except now it wasn't Charlotte and Dylan. It was just Charlotte, who was looking toward the forest.

"Where's Dylan?" Billy exclaimed.

"Dylan!" Charlotte shouted. "Dylan, this isn't funny! Get back here."

Silence.

"What do we do?" said Charlotte uneasily. "Should we go back to camp? Maybe we should get help."

"We can't just leave them," said Billy.

Then he heard a yell that sounded distinctly like Dylan.

It was coming from . . . No, that couldn't be right. It sounded like it was *inside* the mountain. "Dylan!" Charlotte shouted, running toward the small triangular opening at the base, her long hair flying out behind her. "Dylan, are you in there?"

"Charlotte, wait!" cried Billy, going after her. The strangeness of yesterday came flooding back, stronger than before.

He felt another gust of wind, and a long shining silver blur shot out from the gap in the rock. It wrapped around Charlotte and pulled her into the mountain with it.

Billy froze in his tracks. He took a deep breath and began to back away from the mountain, keeping his eyes trained on the opening. He could see now that it was just big enough for a person to go through, almost like a small doorway.

He got to the edge of the forest and paused. He realized he was expecting the same thing that had happened to his friends to happen to him. Waiting for that gust of wind.

But nothing. Just silence.

He knew his friends were in that mountain, and he knew that something—something fast and strong—had taken them.

Billy stared at the mountain and could have sworn that the mountain stared back. Or, at least, something in the mountain stared back.

His palms started sweating, and his heart beat faster than ever. He put a hand on a tree to steady himself. He was afraid. He was alone. He could turn back, or he could do the brave thing. Do what in his heart he knew he wanted to do.

He made a decision. He wasn't going to wait around for that thing to come and get him.

And he wasn't going to leave his friends either.

Billy thought about his family, about home. He looked up at the wall of limestone in front of him, realizing that if he went in, he might not ever come out. From deep in the mountain, he heard a faint cry. And Billy knew what he had to do.

He walked into the mountain.

CHAPTER 12
A DISCOVERY OF DRAGONS

It was dark inside the mountain. Dark and surprisingly cool. Billy found himself in a tunnel. He guessed that the light from the entrance would be enough for a little bit, but he didn't know how deep the tunnel went.

Or if there were any sheer drops or sharp turns.

He strained his ears. All he could hear now was the steady dripping of something up ahead. His friends *had* to be in here. Somewhere. He'd find them.

Billy took slow and steady steps into the heart of the mountain. He glanced over his shoulder. The entrance and the sunlight looked a long way away. He wasn't sure what he was going to do when the light faded.

And then he reached a dead end—a solid gray wall. Billy paused, overwhelmed with sudden fear and confusion. He clenched his fists to keep his hands from shaking. How could his friends have just disappeared? He'd *seen* Charlotte being pulled in here. Where was she?

Maybe he should turn back and get help after all. He was way out of his depth.

In frustration, he kicked at the wall in front of him.

His foot went straight through.

It wasn't a wall at all but a thick gray mist that only looked like a wall. Billy put his hands out, and they disappeared in the mist. He swallowed and looked back again. He had a feeling that if he didn't go through the mist, his friends wouldn't make it out. They needed him, and there wasn't any more time to waste. Summoning as much courage as he could, he took a deep breath and stepped into the mist, his hands out in front of him. He couldn't see at all. The floor sloped beneath his feet, and he tumbled forward.

When he got to his feet, he saw that he was in an enormous cavern with thousands of glowing crystals all along the walls. As his eyes adjusted to the flickering light, he gasped. Because in front of him were Charlotte, Ling-Fei, and Dylan.

And they weren't alone.

His three friends stood with their backs to each other, in a protective triangular stance. Circling around them, in a blur of silver and gold, was a long and slender *dragon*.

Old Gold's legend about the mountain was true.

Dragons were *real*. Billy's heart began to beat very quickly. All those times he'd looked to the sky with Eddie, hoping for a glimpse of dragons, and here they were. Inside this mountain.

And holding his friends captive.

His wonder quickly faded as he realized with a jolt that real dragons meant real danger.

The dragon seemed to sense Billy's presence, and it stopped circling but stayed hovering in the air. Billy saw now that although its long body was looped around his friends at least four times, it still had length to spare. It raised its large head and stared at Billy with glowing silver eyes. Billy stared back. The dragon had a serpentine face, small elegant horns, long whiskers, and scales that fanned out from its neck and behind its ears. Farther down its body, small, gossamer-thin wings moved slowly, as if they were under water. And there, clutched in one of its claws, was Ling-Fei's necklace.

Billy's heart hammered in his chest, and his vision blurred. He thought he might pass out.

The dragon's pink forked tongue flicked out between a sharp set of teeth. It flared its nostrils, and two jets of fire shot out, close enough for Billy to feel the heat on his face.

"Billy! Watch out!" shouted Dylan, noticing him now that the dragon had turned its attention on Billy. But they were still trapped.

Billy took a step back. This was worse than being pummeled by a wave, worse than the tiger. He thrust his hands in his pockets, looking for something to use to defend himself, but all he felt was an old train ticket stub, the lucky seashell he always carried, and a few pennies.

Suddenly, the dragon lunged forward, wrapped itself around Billy, and hoisted him in the air. Billy fought as hard as he could, punching down on the dragon's hard scales and trying to kick himself free. The dragon let out an ear-splitting roar and tightened its grip. Billy couldn't move his arms or legs now, and he could barely breathe. The dragon's hot, smoky breath burned the insides of his nostrils, and he could see all the jagged edges of its teeth.

The dragon flicked its tongue out again, hitting Billy in the face. Its tongue was rough and sticky. Billy wondered for a second whether the dragon was tasting him—deciding if he would make a good meal.

"PUT HIM DOWN!" yelled Charlotte from below. Billy glanced at his friends and saw a rock hurtling toward him. It struck the dragon below its eye and bounced off with little effect. The dragon let out what sounded like a laugh. Billy was starting to feel light-headed. He was losing the feeling in his arms and legs. *This is it*, he thought. *This is going to be the end.*

A scraping sound, like knives being sharpened, came from a corner of the cavern, and *another* dragon emerged from the darkness. Its scales were a river of green and gold, and it walked on its hind legs, like a T-rex. It had small green wings sprouting from its back and an unexpectedly big, round belly that swayed in front of it as its thick tail dragged behind. It clinked its claws together, as if applauding.

Without warning, the silver dragon let go of Billy. He hit the cave floor with a thud.

"Run, Billy!" shouted Dylan. "Get out while you can!"

"I'm not leaving you guys!" Billy cried between gasping breaths. His mind was working in overdrive. The tiger had disappeared when they'd been together. He remembered the jolt he'd felt when they'd held hands. He'd thought that had been a surge of adrenaline. But maybe it was something more. Maybe it was some kind of magic that had made the tiger disappear. Maybe all he needed to do was reach his friends, and the dragons would disappear, too.

His heart pounding in his chest, Billy ran toward Dylan, Charlotte, and Ling-Fei.

He had almost reached them when out of the shadows, another dragon swooped in front of him. Billy slipped and landed hard on his back. He scuttled backward like a crab, keeping his eyes on the dragon. This one was a pale, shimmery blue with flecks of gold. Sharp gold antlers rose from its diamond-shaped head. It had a long neck that curved into its seahorse-like body and a long, narrow tail. An electric blue mane ran from its head all along its spine to the end of its tail. Huge sheer wings that looked like giant bat wings kept it afloat. It seemed to emit its own light, and the air crackled around its body.

The blue dragon stared at him. Billy tried to keep from trembling, but he could feel his knees shaking. He felt like he'd swallowed a huge stone. Dragons. Real dragons. If he ever made it home, he'd have to tell Eddie that they were even more amazing and terrifying than they ever imagined. But he wasn't sure he'd ever make it back. He closed his eyes, trying to block everything out, trying to work out what to do next. If he couldn't get to his friends, maybe he could—

Something tugged on his hand. His eyes flew open, and he saw Charlotte had somehow slipped through the silver dragon's coils. Dylan and Ling-Fei were still trapped.

"Come on," Charlotte said breathlessly, "We've got to go get help."

They raced past the blue dragon, which stared at them with its unnerving, unwavering gaze. The green dragon with the long claws dove at them as they passed but missed, not quite fast enough.

"How'd you get in here?" Charlotte asked as they ran. "I can't find a way out!"

Billy looked around, trying to figure out which way he'd come in.

The silver dragon shot toward them now, knocking Ling-Fei and Dylan over in a heap on the floor. Charlotte yanked Billy out of the way, and they raced in the other direction.

From deeper in the cavern came a low rumble. Smoke filled the air. A pair of red eyes lit up in the darkness. The floor trembled as a new dragon approached from the shadows. By far the biggest dragon yet, it looked like it had been through hundreds of battles. Its body was a tapestry of scars and red and gold scales.

And it was coming right toward them.

CHAPTER 13
SUPERIOR TO HUMANS

The giant red dragon roared so loudly that Billy thought the entire mountain might come down on their heads. It hunched on its front paws and unleashed a stream of fire that hit the wall ahead of Billy and Charlotte. They turned, running from the flames and back toward Dylan and Ling-Fei. The red dragon slowly pivoted its head so the flames chased them, licking at their heels.

Billy and Charlotte reached the center of the cavern and lunged for their friends. The four quickly threw their arms around each other, solid proof that they were there, alive, and that this was actually happening. Then they turned to face out, each one like the sentry of a different direction on a compass.

For a moment, Billy hoped his theory was right—that now the four of them were together, the dragons would disappear as the tiger had. Instead the dragons moved closer.

The red dragon blew a stream of fire around them, circling them—trapping them. Billy and his friends instinctively moved closer together, tightening their stance. The heat of the flames was fiercer than anything Billy had ever felt. And there was no way out.

"What now?" Dylan whispered, adjusting his glasses very slowly.

Billy stared at the blue dragon. Its eyes locked on to his. Billy felt an unexpected calm descend on him. It was like he was in a dream or outside his body watching what was happening. He knew that they couldn't defeat the dragons.

But he also knew, with a sudden sharp clarity, that if the dragons had wanted to kill them, he and his friends would be dead already.

This felt more like . . .

A test of some kind.

"I think," Billy murmured hesitantly, "I think we should try to communicate with them. Dragons are meant to be smart, right?"

"Dragons aren't meant to exist," said Dylan. "And I'm pretty sure, in my limited knowledge of them, that they are *man-eating monsters*."

"I agree with Billy," whispered Ling-Fei. "The silver one has my necklace! That can't be a coincidence."

She nodded to where the silver one watched them, Ling-Fei's jade necklace swaying from its front claws.

"We should find out what they want," said Charlotte.

"What if what they want is to *eat us*?" said Dylan.

"If they want to eat us, they are going to eat us no matter what," said Billy. "If we try to communicate with them, we might have a shot at surviving."

As the friends muttered among themselves, the dragons pressed closer. Billy thought he saw something like curiosity alight in their eyes. The blue dragon blew a stream of cold air at the flames surrounding them, turning the fire to a wall of ice.

They were still trapped, but no longer at risk of being barbecued.

As Billy wondered how they should try to talk to the dragons, Dylan suddenly cried, "DON'T EAT US!"

The green dragon began to slap its short arms together, claws clanking, and bared its teeth in what looked like a terrifying grin. Did it . . . Could it . . . ?

"Can you understand us?" Billy shouted. "Do you want something from us?"

The dragons looked at each other. And then Billy knew for sure that they could understand what he and his friends were saying.

The silver dragon flew over the wall of ice, slithering down next to them. The friends pressed even closer together.

"You are not what we were expecting," it said in a smooth and hypnotic voice.

"You . . . you can speak?" Billy stammered. However he had imagined communicating with the dragons, he had *not* expected this.

The silver dragon smirked. That was the only word for its expression. "Of course we speak, human fool. We are superior to humans in every way imaginable—don't you think we would also master your simple tongue?"

Ling-Fei burst out in Mandarin, speaking so quickly Billy couldn't understand her.

The silver dragon responded in kind.

"What did you ask it?" Billy whispered.

"Don't bother whispering," the silver dragon said. "We have incredibly advanced hearing. If we focus enough, we can even hear your heartbeats."

Billy wondered how loud his own heartbeat was.

"Your friend asked me about her necklace," the silver dragon went on. "Why I have it. She seems not to know just how valuable it is."

"My grandmother gave it to me," Ling-Fei said in a fierce voice. "It means more to me than it does to you."

The silver dragon whipped its long tail against the ice wall, shattering it.

Billy ducked and shielded his face from shards of flying ice, as did Charlotte and Dylan. But Ling-Fei stood unflinchingly amid the ice shards and fearlessly faced the silver dragon.

"The necklace is not what interests me," the silver dragon hissed. "I only care about *this*." With one sharp claw, the silver dragon plucked the jade stone from the necklace setting. "Here," it said, tossing the necklace around Ling-Fei's neck like a lasso.

Ling-Fei's hands shot up, and she clutched the now-empty necklace. "Give that back," she demanded.

"Least of our worries, Ling-Fei," Dylan said in a low voice.

"Give me my jade stone back and let us go," Ling-Fei said, louder this time.

"You should have been more careful with the necklace," the silver dragon taunted. Then it sighed. "Though I'm glad you dropped it, so you had reason to return."

"You *wanted* us to come back?" asked Billy. Something began to dawn on him. "You need us for something," he said slowly. "That's why you've trapped us here. That's why you captured my friends in the first place. And why you haven't killed us." He steeled himself. "Tell us why we're here."

CHAPTER 14
THE DRAGON OF DEATH

"I suppose we owe you that much," said the silver dragon.

"We owe them more than that!" The green dragon spoke for the first time.

"After all, you opened the mountain," said the dragon with the sparkling blue mane in a surprisingly soft voice.

"We did?" asked Billy. He didn't think anything could surprise him at this point, but he hadn't expected that.

"But it isn't enough!" snapped the silver one.

"They are the ones we've been waiting for!" said the green dragon. "Haven't we tested them sufficiently? They are brave, loyal, strong, and true! And working together! If they weren't . . . well, they would still be outside doing whatever it is humans are doing in this age, and we'd still be stuck in here."

"We'll still be stuck in here unless we can convince them to cooperate," hissed the silver dragon.

"Then maybe *you* should be more cooperative!" huffed the green one.

"SILENCE!" roared the red dragon. Hot sulfuric breath rushed over them, stinging Billy's eyes.

"I must be dreaming," said Dylan, sounding a bit dazed. "This can't be happening. None of this. Dragons don't talk." He started to laugh, a little hysterically. "Dragons don't *exist*."

Charlotte reached over and pinched Dylan on the arm. Hard.

"Ow!" he said, rubbing his arm. "What did you do that for?"

"To show you that this *is* happening. Now pull yourself together!" She turned to look up at the dragons. "What do you mean, you've been waiting for us?"

"We've been trapped inside this mountain for many years," the blue dragon said. "Waiting for four humans to come and open it." The dragon smiled. "Although we didn't expect you to be so young."

"Little more than hatchlings," said the silver dragon with a sneer.

"But with your youth comes pure hearts, and that will help us all," the blue dragon went on.

The friends looked at each other and back at the dragons. "What *exactly* do you need us for?" said Billy.

"Food, probably," muttered Dylan, moving slightly behind Billy.

"Please," sniffed the silver dragon. "You'd barely be a snack."

"Stop antagonizing the humans," said the green dragon. "That isn't the way to get them on our side."

"And what side is that?" said Ling-Fei.

"Yeah, because if it is dragons versus humans, we are definitely on the human side," said Billy, with as much bravado as he could muster.

"It is a question of good versus evil," said the red dragon.

"Pretty sure that fire-breathing, man-eating dragons aren't on the good side," said Dylan.

"We like to avoid eating humans," said the green dragon. It gave a sly glance at the huge red dragon. "Even him, despite what he might want you to think."

"So what do you mean by good versus evil?" asked Billy.

"Let us explain. It might be easier to show you," said the blue dragon, taking a deep breath and blowing frosted air on the wall behind them. Pictures began to appear in the ice, of dragons and humans and mountains. "There are two realms that exist in this world. The Human Realm, which you know, and the Dragon Realm, where we are from. This mountain you stand in now is one of the only passages between the two realms, and it has been sealed shut for"—the blue dragon paused, calculating—"at least one hundred human years, maybe more. We used to be the guardians of all that passed through, human or dragon."

"Why would dragons want to come into the human world?" asked Billy.

"I told you," whispered Dylan, "to eat us."

"Because one of the greatest ways for a dragon to gain power is to form a bond with a human," said the red dragon. "Not any human, you understand. Only a human with a heart that matches its own." The images on the ice showed a dragon flying with a human on its back.

The green dragon stepped forward. "One dragon, an evil dragon known as the Dragon of Death, sought to enter the human realm to find a heart as evil as her own and use her powers to rule over all dragons and humans across both realms. We had a great battle in this very mountain. Much blood was spilled." The images on the ice changed, showing one dragon slaying other dragons until their bodies piled up.

"The river of dragon blood," said Ling-Fei in awe. "It's true."

The silver dragon snapped its head around. "How do you know about that?"

"It's an old legend," said Ling-Fei. "I should have known that all legends have a hint of truth."

"How did you defeat the Dragon of Death?" asked Billy.

"We didn't," said the red dragon flatly. "She is the reason we are stuck in this mountain. We managed to create a time portal to an age before humans and before dragons, but as we sent her back, she cast a curse to seal us in this mountain until we found four hearts that matched our own."

"So, we've done that?" said Charlotte, staring at the dragons. "You mean *our* hearts match *your* hearts?"

"It appears so," said the green dragon. "Otherwise you wouldn't have opened the mountain."

"It was only after you came to the mountain, together, that it opened enough for me to slip out and grab three of you. We needed to know that you were loyal, which is why we left one of you to decide what to do for yourself," said the silver dragon.

"Does the disappearing tiger we saw have anything to do with this curse?" said Billy.

"A disappearing tiger?" repeated the green dragon, drumming its claws on its jaw. "Intriguing. Tigers and dragons don't usually get along, you know."

"A tiger chased us here, and when we thought it was going to attack us, it just . . . disappeared," explained Ling-Fei.

The dragons looked at each other.

"Perhaps it is part of the curse," mused the silver dragon. "But you made it here either despite or because of it."

"And opening the mountain is only the start of what we need from you," said the red dragon.

"We'd hoped that by sending the Dragon of Death through the time portal, she would be lost in time forever. But she is returning," said the blue dragon. "I am a seer dragon. I can see into the past and into the future, and I have seen the return of the Dragon of Death. She is even stronger than before. And she will bring devastation in both realms." It turned its bright blue eyes toward the children. "We need your help to get into the Dragon Realm and to stop the Dragon of Death for good."

CHAPTER 15
FOUR HEARTS

"I think there must be some sort of mistake," said Dylan. He turned to Billy, Ling-Fei, and Charlotte. "No offense, but I don't think we're the ones to help defeat something called the *Dragon of Death*."

"You opened the mountain. You wouldn't have been able to do that if you weren't the ones foretold to break the curse," said the blue dragon.

"Foretold to do . . . what exactly?" said Billy. He couldn't imagine that the four of them, four kids, could do anything useful to help four giant, fire-breathing dragons. And yet here they stood, talking to dragons. If that was possible, *anything* was possible.

"You are wise to be hesitant," said the green dragon. "What we are asking of you is no small thing. We are asking you to join a war. To fight. To save both your world and our own."

Dylan audibly gulped.

"And if we say no?" said Ling-Fei softly.

"The Dragon of Death will return. She will destroy both realms," said the red dragon. It turned to the blue dragon. "Tell them what you've seen."

The blue dragon closed its eyes. "The Dragon of Death has an unquenchable thirst for power. She will kill humans and dragons alike. In the future I have seen, evil and chaos reign under her rule. Her followers will rise up, poisoned by their desire to share in her dark power. There is a name for those who betray all that is good to join the Dragon of Death—the Noxious."

"Otherwise known as the nox-wings," said the green dragon grimly.

"They spread devastation wherever they go," continued the blue dragon, its eyes now open. "The Dragon of Death and her nox-wings will enslave humans and dragons for her own dark devices. Your world will be unrecognizable in its devastation." The images on the ice behind the blue dragon shifted again, showing a world in chaos—humans and dragons in chains, all lorded over by a dragon wrapped around a tall spire, its head thrown back in triumph.

Billy shivered.

"So . . . um, if you don't mind me asking, how accurate are these visions?" asked Dylan. "The future is kind of wobbly, isn't it? Like, if you said I was going to be hit by a car tomorrow, I just wouldn't cross any roads." He paused. "I realize you might not know what a car is— it's this thing with wheels . . . oh, man, do you know what wheels are?" He looked at Billy. "I chose the wrong metaphor."

"I think what Dylan is trying to say," said Billy, a smile twitching at his lips despite the fact that they were face to face with fire-breathing dragons who had just told them an even more dangerous dragon was going to end the world as they knew it, "is that the future is changeable, isn't it?"

"I understand what you are asking," said the blue dragon. "I see many visions. There are countless variations of the future. All depending on the choices we make now." The blue dragon looked at each of them. "I have seen what will happen if the Dragon of Death is not defeated. It is an accurate vision of what will come unless . . ."

"Unless we help you," Billy said. He kept his voice steady even though he was reeling from everything.

"Precisely," said the green dragon.

"And how are we meant to help you?" Billy went on, still trying to get his head around what the dragons wanted.

"We're asking each of you to accept the rare and ancient dragon-human bond that can only happen when a human heart matches one of a dragon," said the blue dragon. "We already know your four hearts match ours, but that is not enough. It is the bond itself that will allow us, all of us together, to change the dark destiny I foresee. But you should know this—only death can break the bond between a human and their dragon. It is no small thing to take on."

"We cannot force you to accept the bond," said the green dragon.

"Unfortunately," muttered the silver one. "That would make this all much easier."

"Ignore her," said the green dragon with what looked like an attempt at a smile.

"The bond must be initiated with a willing heart," said the red dragon. "But if you do accept the dragon bond, together we will be strong enough to fight the Dragon of Death. And you four will be able to join the battle, tipping the scales in our favor."

"What do you think?" said the blue dragon.

"Sounds like we are going to get fried by dragons either way," said Billy slowly. "I guess it's a question of if we want to try to *do* anything about it or just wait it out." As he said the words, he wondered what he wanted to do. Fighting alongside dragons sounded exciting in theory. But did he really think he could survive in a dragon war? He thought about his parents, his brother. Would he ever see them again? Then he remembered the images on the ice wall. And he knew he'd do whatever it took to stop anything bad from ever happening to his family.

"I can see the appeal of waiting it out," admitted Dylan. "In my own bed. Cozy. Ideally sleeping when all this devastation happens. Wouldn't notice a thing."

Charlotte rolled her eyes. "Don't be such a chicken."

"You *want* to do this? Go fight *dragons?*" said Dylan. "Super-powerful, evil dragons?"

"I'd rather go down swinging than just lie down and let someone stomp all over me," said Charlotte. "And it isn't like it would just be us versus dragons. We'd be fighting *with* dragons."

The red dragon let out a snort that might have been a laugh. "I like your fire," it said.

Billy ran his hand through his hair. "Charlotte's right," he said.

"She is?" said Dylan incredulously.

"I am?" said Charlotte.

"I think so, too," said Ling-Fei.

"We can't go back to camp, back to our old lives, and pretend none of this happened," Billy went on. "We have to do whatever we can to help stop this future from happening." Here was a chance to do something extraordinary. The chance to be a hero. To do something that would make his family, make *everyone*, proud. And, on top of that, he knew he would never forgive himself if he missed out on an adventure like this. He looked up at the dragons. "And you're sure it's the four of us?"

"The combination of four hearts coming together that match our own is rare. We have been waiting a long time," said the red dragon.

"I mean, this mountain is kind of in the middle of nowhere. No wonder you've been waiting so long," said Dylan.

"Don't be insolent," hissed the silver dragon. "The curse cannot be fooled. It *has* to be you four. Even you, despite your constant mewling."

Dylan took a small step back, eyes wide behind his glasses. "Understood."

"It is your choice now," said the green dragon.

"I want to help you," said Ling-Fei, her eyes shining.

"Me, too," said Charlotte.

Billy turned to his friends. "Aren't you guys scared? This sounds huge. Huger than huge." He wanted to say yes, wanted to go do this world-changing, world-saving thing. But that didn't mean the idea of it didn't terrify him.

"Of course," said Charlotte. "But just because something scares you isn't a reason to not do it."

Billy nodded. He knew what she meant. He got a little scared every time he took on a wave bigger than he had before. Every time he entered a surf competition. But he was always glad he did it. And this—this was so much more epic than anything he'd ever done or even imagined he'd ever do.

"Nothing is certain," said Ling-Fei. "But at least we'll be together.

And that was when it clicked inside Billy, like a puzzle piece being snapped into place. He remembered when they'd faced the tiger outside the mountain. How it was something about their very togetherness that seemed to save them.

"I'm in," said Billy. A mix of fear and excitement shot from his fingertips all the way to his toes, sending a warmth buzzing through him.

"All right, all right," said Dylan. "I can't be the one who says no and dooms all of mankind and dragonkind. I'm in, too."

Billy grinned at his friend. "We couldn't do it without you, Dylan." Then he looked up at the dragons. "Is that it? Are we bonded now?"

"Not quite," said the blue dragon with a smile. "But

I'm heartened you want to accept the bond and all that comes with it."

"Your willingness to accept shows you four do indeed have the kind of bravery and loyalty that we will need for the battle ahead," said the red dragon. "But there are steps to initiating and cementing the bond."

"Is there some kind of official dragon-human bonding ceremony?" said Charlotte. "I love a ceremony."

The green dragon grinned, its teeth sharp and glinting. "First things first. As you have now committed to accepting the bond, we should show you our hoards."

"Your hoards?" said Dylan. "Like treasure?"

"Exactly like treasure! All dragons hoard," the green dragon went on. "And if we are going to be working together, you should get to know us better. A dragon's hoard is their most precious thing and gives excellent insight into their personality and their hearts.

"Which is why my hoard is the most impressive and your hoard is . . . well . . . not," said the silver dragon.

"We do not have time to argue about the merits of our hoards," said the red dragon. "But I agree, it is important for the children to see them."

"Follow me," sang the silver dragon, floating by in the air.

Billy and his friends looked at each other. "You guys sure about this?" said Billy.

"Please," said Charlotte, tossing her hair. "It's just seeing some treasure. *This* isn't the bit we should be scared about. *This* is the fun bit. Come on." She strode after the silver dragon.

"She's got a point," said Ling-Fei, hurrying after Charlotte.

"Wait up! We should stay together!" Billy called after them.

"You all are definitely, one hundred percent going to get me killed," said Dylan.

"You don't sound too upset by that," said Billy, nudging him.

"If you've got to go, death by dragons seems a pretty good way to go," said Dylan with a wry grin.

Billy laughed and shook his head. "This . . . it is all a bit unbelievable, isn't it?"

"I figure as long as you guys are seeing the same stuff I am, at least I'm not going completely bonkers," said Dylan cheerfully.

"Hurry up!" Charlotte yelled from up ahead. "You guys will want to see this!"

Billy and Dylan raced after the others, going down a long corridor. Shimmering crystals overhead lit their way.

At the end of the corridor, Billy had to shield his eyes.

Diamonds, some as big as baseballs, shone next to glistening emeralds. Red rubies winked in the light. A whole stack of jade bracelets towered so tall it almost touched the ceiling of the cavern. There were necklaces and earrings, pendants and rings. The silver dragon flew around her hoard with pride and then dove headfirst into it, sending jewels and gems flying.

The children stared, openmouthed.

"Well," said the silver dragon, popping her head out from her sparkling pile of jewels. "What do you think?"

"It's incredible," said Ling-Fei, her dark eyes reflecting the shine of the jewels.

"It's like something out of a dream," said Billy. "Where did you get it all?"

"Oh, I've been growing it for years and years, little hatchling."

"Can we go to my hoard now?" asked the green dragon, bouncing up and down.

"I don't know why he's in such a hurry to embarrass himself," sniffed the silver one.

"I will leave it to the humans to judge," said the green dragon.

"I'd very much like to see your hoard," said Dylan. He took off his glasses and wiped them on his shirt. "I'll admit, I'm not sure how it could be more impressive than this one."

"You wait," said the green dragon with a wink. "It's just this way," He walked around the silver dragon's pile of jewels and down another corridor. The cavern crystals flickered to life above them as they moved deeper into the lair.

"This," said the green dragon, waving his small arms out grandly, "is *my* hoard."

Billy instantly understood why the silver dragon had mocked the green dragon.

There was not a shining jewel in sight. The green dragon's hoard appeared to be a heap of . . . junk.

"I only collect human-made items," said the green

dragon proudly. "Buttons, especially. So easily confused with coins, don't you think? I often wonder how humans tell them apart!"

"Tell buttons apart from money?" asked Billy, stepping forward to take a closer look at the green dragon's hoard.

Everywhere he looked, there were hundreds—no, thousands—of multicolored buttons, of all sizes and materials. Where had the dragon found all of these?

"Yes! I think my buttons are worth far more. They are all so different! Why would anyone want, say, a stack of identical gold coins"—he shot a sly look in the direction of the red dragon—"when they could have a stack of unique buttons?" He bit his lip and looked anxiously around. "You do agree, don't you?"

Billy blinked, unsure what to say. He had a sneaking suspicion that it was a bad idea to lie to a dragon, but he also didn't want to offend him . . .

"I love your buttons!" said a voice from behind him. It was Dylan. "I am a fan of buttons myself."

"Oh, thank you!" said the green dragon, beaming.

"Enough about buttons," said the red dragon. "Do you want to see some real treasure? Come, follow me to *my* hoard." The dragon turned and lumbered down another corridor, leaving smoky air in his wake.

Billy wondered what the red dragon considered "real treasure" to be. Part of him worried that it might be human skeletons or something equally terrifying.

Charlotte seemed to have no such worries. "Come on!" she said. "I bet this one really does have the best hoard."

As they turned down the corridor to where the red dragon waited, Billy stopped in his tracks, amazed. Floating orange balls of flame lit up the cavern. And there were piles and piles of gold coins, all spilling over each other and tinkling as they did. Towers of gold bars reached the roof of the cavern. Gold crowns and necklaces and rings. Candelabras and gold shoes and even a gold throne. All glowing yellow gold.

"Wow!" said Charlotte, her eyes huge. "Can I try on that crown?"

"Maybe another time," said the red dragon.

Billy looked up at the blue dragon. "Where's your hoard?"

The blue dragon looked bashful. "Mine doesn't compare to these hoards. It's . . . different."

"Her hoard is very special," said the green dragon. "Unique. Not quite my taste, but special."

"I'd like to see it," said Billy, intrigued.

"We have to go deeper in the cavern. Stay close," said the blue dragon.

As they wound deeper through the mountain, the air around them grew damp and cool.

Finally, something glinted up ahead.

"It's a waterfall!" said Ling-Fei, squinting in the darkness. "A glowing waterfall!"

"Indeed it is. And my hoard is behind it," said the blue dragon. She flew forward on her silent wings and then lifted one wing under the waterfall, like an umbrella. "This way."

Billy went first and found himself in a tiny grotto lit

by glowing blue icicles hanging from the ceiling. In the center was a small pool. It was full of beautiful shells and shining rocks and brightly colored coral.

"I have more of a . . . living hoard," said the blue dragon. She ran a wing in the water and the pool lit up. "There's some stardust in there, too."

"It's like a tide pool," said Billy, crouching down to watch glowing green seagrass waving just below the surface of the water. Then he straightened, reaching into his pocket to wrap his hand around his lucky seashell. Pearly white and shaped like a clamshell, its edges had softened with time. He held it out. "Would you like to add this to your hoard?" he asked. "It looks like you already have a lot of shells, but this one is from California, which is pretty far from here."

"It is very kind of you to give me something from your home," said the blue dragon. "Thank you." She gently took the shell from Billy's outstretched hand with her teeth and dropped it in the glowing pool. As the shell struck the water, it took on its own shimmering light.

Billy looked at the blue dragon. "I'm . . . your match, aren't I?" he said, feeling a bit dizzy with the hugeness of it all. He was filled with a thrumming electric pulse.

The blue dragon dipped her head. "I'm glad you can feel it, too."

"What happens now?" asked Billy.

"Hold on a second," said Charlotte. "What about us? We need to match with our dragons!"

"So impatient," said the silver dragon, and Billy could have sworn she rolled her eyes. "Of course you will match with your dragon. That is the entire point of you being here."

"Let's go back up to our main cavern," said the red dragon. "It's far too cold down here. And it's time to initiate the dragon bond."

CHAPTER 16
THE POWER OF A NAME

Billy's heart hammered as he stood with his friends across from the dragons.

Not from fear. From excitement.

"Before we go forward, we want to make sure you know what you are committing to," said the red dragon. "By accepting the dragon bond, you will be forever tied to us—even across the realms. You will feel our pain and our joy, and when we are separated, you will feel like something is missing."

"He's right," said the blue dragon. "But also, when we are near, you will feel a sense of wholeness you have never known before."

"When a dragon has a matching heart with a human, that human names the dragon," the red dragon went on. "It is the first step in cementing the dragon and human bond. I've had several names in my time. When

99

our humans die, so does the name. It is wiped from my memory and all who have ever spoken it."

"We always remember the humans we bond with, though," said the green dragon, sounding a bit wistful.

"Such short life spans," said the silver dragon, shaking her head. "So easily killed. It's a shame that we can't bond with stronger creatures."

"Ignore her," said the green dragon. "She's never appreciated humans."

"So who is bonding with who?" asked Ling-Fei. "We have to know that before we can name you, right?"

"Can't you feel which of us has a heart to match your own?" said the blue dragon. "I know Billy has." Billy stood a little taller, proud he'd already recognized which dragon was his.

Charlotte stepped forward. "You," she said, pointing at the big red dragon. "You're my dragon." The red dragon chuckled. "Only a human of extraordinary bravery would dare to claim me."

"Well, that sounds like me," said Charlotte, standing her ground. She looked the red dragon directly in the eye.

Billy suddenly remembered just how vulnerable he and the others were. These were *dragons*. With teeth and claws that could strike them down in a second. Billy moved closer to Charlotte so she would know that he had her back. Even against dragons.

"I'll prove my bravery," said Charlotte. Her whole body was thrumming with energy, like she was gearing up for something. "I name you Tank," she said. Then she took a deep breath and leapt up onto his nose, scrambling up until she was sitting on his head. "And you are my dragon!"

The red dragon roared and rose to his full height, taking Charlotte with it.

"Hold on, Charlotte!" Billy shouted. He felt helpless down on the ground, and even though he wasn't the one up in the air, his stomach had dropped into his shoes.

But Charlotte had her own plan. "I trust you, Tank!" she said. With a wild yell, she jumped off the top of the red dragon's head and plummeted toward the cavern floor.

Before any of them could move, the red dragon shot his arm out and caught Charlotte in the pad of his paw. Her long blond hair dangled between his claws.

"That was *incredibly* irresponsible," huffed the red dragon, gently tipping Charlotte out on the floor. Then he grinned a little. "You have good instincts," he said gruffly.

"I know," said Charlotte.

"Tank," mused the red dragon. "I suppose that is an acceptable name." Beneath his scales, his heart began to glow, and he grew even bigger, until his head brushed the top of the cavern. His scales thickened like armored plates, and his claws and horns lengthened. He closed his eyes, and when they opened, they had turned from red to gold.

"It's because you look like a tank," said Charlotte. "Nothing could stop you." She stared up at him. "Especially now! What . . . what just happened?"

"It's the bond," said Tank. "We grow stronger in ability, but also physically. Naming me would have been enough, but I appreciate your show of bravery and trust in me."

"It was foolhardy," said the silver dragon. "*My* human would never do such a thing." She turned to Ling-Fei. "You are far too wise for something like that. I can sense it."

Ling-Fei blushed.

Billy looked back and forth between the silver dragon and Ling-Fei. Ling-Fei had such a kind heart; even after knowing her for only a few days, he could tell that. Was the silver dragon hiding a kind heart beneath her spiky exterior?

"I've been thinking about your name," said Ling-Fei. "I bet, when you fly in the night sky, not just in a cave, you shine like a star."

"It's been a long time since any of us have flown in a sky," said the silver dragon.

"I'd like to see it one day," said Ling-Fei.

"You have a poet's heart," said the silver dragon approvingly. "Poets of old have written about us. When we used to show ourselves to the worthy. Perhaps you will be the poet of your time."

Ling-Fei's face lit up. "I love poetry," she admitted. "May I give you your name now?"

"It would be an honor."

"Xing," said Ling-Fei, pronouncing it like *shing*. "It's—"

"The Chinese word for star," said the silver dragon. "Do you like it?"

"I do."

And as Ling-Fei and Xing gazed at each other, a golden light enveloped them. Xing's scales began to shine like the jewels in her hoard, and her jaw extended. She grinned, showing newly sharpened teeth made of diamonds. Like Tank, her eyes changed to glowing gold.

Xing writhed with pleasure. "Oh, to be strong again," she said. "It feels delicious."

"Do stop showing off," said the green dragon. "It is making me frightfully jealous."

Dylan stepped forward. "No need to be jealous, my friend. You must be my dragon," he said.

The green dragon howled with delight. "Yes! Yes, I am! I knew as soon as you came into the mountain that you were my human." He opened his eyes wide. "Do you have a name for me?"

"What about . . ." Dylan grinned, tugged a button off his shirt and held it out as an offering. "Buttons?"

Before Billy realized what was happening, the green dragon had reached out with his short arms, clutched Dylan against his big belly, and spun around in a circle.

"Buttons!" howled the green dragon. "It's perfect!" A fat tear of happiness rolled out of the corner of his eye. He put Dylan down, who looked shocked and rumpled but more or less all right with what had just happened, and turned to the other dragons. "Hello, I'm Buttons," he said with a deep bow. As he straightened, his heart glowed gold beneath his scales, and huge spikes erupted from his back. His chest and belly extended, and his tail grew thick behind him. He blinked, and his eyes, too, had turned to gold.

"You were right," he said to Xing. "It *is* delicious."

Everyone turned expectantly to Billy and the blue dragon. Even though Billy was the last to name his dragon, he was pleased he had been the first to recognize their bond.

"Are you ready to give me a name?" asked the blue dragon hopefully.

Billy tentatively reached out and stroked her translucent wing. Small sparks flickered beneath his fingertips like tiny fireflies.

Billy looked up at the dragon, *his* dragon, and smiled. "How do you feel about Spark?"

The blue dragon responded by flying up in the air. Her wings extended even farther, growing and growing, and waves of blue light streamed from her scales. Her mane lengthened and began to glow a vivid electric blue, and her bright blue eyes morphed to gold. A gold ray of light ran from her heart to Billy's.

As it did, Billy felt a jolt go through him, like he'd been electrocuted, but in a good way. He felt all of Spark's joy at being bonded, her pride at being stronger.

"Thank you," said Spark, floating back down to the ground. "I love it."

"So that's it?" said Billy, looking around at the others and wondering if they all felt what he did. Elated and excited and ready for anything. "We're dragon-bonded now?"

"The bond is just the beginning," said Tank.

CHAPTER 17
THE EIGHT PEARLS

"Joining us is not without risks," said Spark. "We cannot promise you will come out of it alive."

Billy's stomach tightened. The thought had occurred to him earlier, but hearing the dragons say it out loud made it so much more real.

"We won't be bringing you into battle completely unprepared," said Tank. "You will also be strengthened by the bond."

"There's another important thing that needs to happen before we go into the Dragon Realm," said Xing. "And I think you are all going to like this part." She held up the jade stone that had been encased in Ling-Fei's necklace. "Do you have any idea what this is?"

The children all shook their heads.

"I just know it was my grandma's," said Ling-Fei.

"I wonder...," said Spark thoughtfully, "I wonder if your grandma knew how valuable it was."

"What do you know about the Eight Great Treasures?" asked Xing.

"I know what they are in Chinese mythology," said Ling-Fei, frowning, "but I thought they were just symbolic."

"Well, *I* didn't think dragons were real," said Dylan. "And here we are."

"The Eight Great Treasures are real," said Xing, "but not in the way you might think. There are eight ancient pearls, each of a different substance. The Flaming Pearl, a pearl glowing with an eternal flame. The Ice Pearl that is always cold and can never be melted. The Lightning Pearl with a storm captured inside it. The Coral Pearl. The Granite Pearl. The Gold Pearl. The Diamond Pearl. And the Jade Pearl. No dragon or human knows exactly where they came from, and we are not sure of their full capabilities. But we do know they provide a measure of protection over the one who carries them. A single pearl won't make you invincible, but it will protect you from harm, to an extent."

She gave Ling-Fei what Billy thought was an attempt at a gentle smile, or as gentle as she could, given her perpetually fierce expression. "Your grandmother might not have known exactly what it was, but I suspect she recognized it as a protective talisman of sorts. By gifting it to you, she's been protecting you even though she isn't here."

Ling-Fei blinked away tears. "It's always sung to me," she said simply. "I feel better when I have it close."

"That isn't all the pearls do," said Buttons, hopping

up and down, barely able to contain his excitement. "Tell them! Tell them!"

"We know that there is power when all eight pearls are together," said Tank, "although I do not know if that has ever happened. The Dragon of Death was trying to find all eight but only managed to locate one."

"Not that!" Buttons burst out. "Tell them the *other* thing about the pearls. The thing they'll want to know."

Billy's eyes darted back and forth between the dragons and the pearl. He didn't think he could be any more excited than he already was, having just bonded with a dragon, but there was something about the way Buttons was talking that had Billy's heart racing even faster.

"When a human who is dragon-bonded has a pearl, the pearl awakens a unique power in the human," said Spark.

"A power?" breathed Billy.

"Are you saying I've been wearing a *magic* pearl for half my life?" said Ling-Fei, her eyes huge.

"Not any magic pearl, but a magic pearl that I once carried," said Xing. "It was lost many years ago, but it sounds like your family has been keeping it safe. And now it has come back to me, just when I need it most. *You* being the one to return it to me makes it all the more valuable. Two treasures instead of one."

Ling-Fei blushed. Billy was surprised to hear Xing so sentimental about both the pearl and Ling-Fei. He wondered if Spark felt like that about him.

"But it *is* magic?" asked Dylan, staring at the pearl.

"You need the dragon bond for it to do anything *really* magical. Only then can the pearl unleash an innate power within the human who holds the pearl," explained Spark.

"So I get . . . a magic power?" Ling-Fei said, staring at the Jade Pearl.

"You *all* get a magic power," said Buttons, sounding delighted. "Dylan, I have the Granite Pearl for you. Nobody expected me to have a pearl, but I've been saving it for many years. Now I can finally bestow it on a human! On my human!"

"And I have the Gold Pearl for you," Tank said to Charlotte. "I have always carried a pearl."

Billy looked expectantly at Spark. She shook her head. "I'm sorry, Billy, I don't have a pearl for you. I once had the Lightning Pearl in my possession, but during our battle with the Dragon of Death, it was lost."

Disappointment washed over Billy like a wave, so strong it almost knocked him down. Would he be the only one without a magic pearl? Without a power to help defeat the Dragon of Death? Could he even survive in the Dragon Realm without one?

"But," Spark quickly went on. "We believe the Lightning Pearl is close. I can't bestow it on you, but you can retrieve it. And then your power will be unlocked."

"What?" exclaimed Billy.

"How do you know it is close?" said Charlotte.

"Xing can sense magic, and because of that she can sense the pearls, the way an animal can track its prey," said Tank. "And she knows this pearl is close."

"It's in the Human Realm," said Xing. "I sensed it when you opened the mountain."

"I think I know where it is," said Billy slowly. A memory was tugging at him. A flashing orb. A storm.

"Slow down," said Dylan. "We *literally* just learned about the existence of these apparently magical pearls, and you somehow know where one is?"

Billy felt his ears get hot. "I might be wrong." Everyone stared at him. He took a deep breath. "The other night, during the storm, I had to go to the bathroom . . ."

"How all great stories begin," said Charlotte.

"Shh! Let him finish," said Ling-Fei. She nodded at Billy encouragingly.

"And when I was walking back, I saw something. Whatever it was, it was letting off its own light. And I thought I saw flashes of lightning around it."

"Billy, buddy, sounds like it could have been a *lot* of things. A lightbulb, a glow-in-the-dark toy, a lamp, a laptop . . ." Dylan listed the items on his fingers as he went. "And where even was it?"

"In the small cabin near the bathrooms," said Billy.

"That's Old Gold's office," said Ling-Fei.

"Who is Old Gold?" asked Xing.

"He's the closest thing I have to a yeye. He runs the camp we're at." She paused. "He loves collecting old artifacts. He might have come across it and not known what it was. Like me with the Jade Pearl."

"Interesting," said Xing. She turned to Billy. "Did it light up like this?" She tapped on the side of the Jade Pearl, and where the thing Billy had seen let out blue sparks of lightning, the Jade Pearl gave off a soft green glow. It was different in color and form, but the effect was remarkably similar.

"Yes!" said Billy.

Ling-Fei stared open mouthed at the glowing Jade Pearl. "How did you do that?" she asked.

"You'll learn," said Xing.

"It sounds like what you saw might very well be the Lightning Pearl," Buttons said. "Do you think you can retrieve it?"

"Definitely," said Billy with more confidence than he felt. "We'll go find the Lightning Pearl and then come back"—he swallowed—"to join you against the Dragon of Death."

"A good plan," said Tank. "But before you go, there is one thing we must do. It's time to unlock your powers."

power is an affinity with the natural world," said Xing. "You can sense things others will not be able to. It is a good power. I am proud. As you should be."

"Charlotte?" prompted Tank.

Charlotte opened and closed her fists. "Well, I certainly can't hear any fish," she said. "But I feel . . ." she paused, "stronger, somehow."

Tank rolled a boulder toward her with his tail. "Lift this," he said.

"There's no way," Billy said under his breath. The boulder was huge, too big even for Charlotte to get her arms all the way around it.

Charlotte squatted down next to the boulder and put her hands beneath it. "I feel silly," she said, looking .

"Just try," said Tank.

Charlotte took a deep breath and lifted the boulder.

"Oh, my stars," she said, so surprised that she dropped it immediately, almost on Dylan's toe. "Did you see that?"

"I should have known strength would be your power," Tank proudly. "It is fitting."

"That's awesome," said Billy, and he meant it. But couldn't help wishing that he had his pearl so he could what *his* power was. He forced the feeling away. about you, Dylan?" he asked.

Dylan clenched his eyes tightly shut and kind of .

Dylan?" Billy asked again, confused.

m waiting," said Dylan. "For it to kick in."

CHAPTER 18
HIDDEN POWERS

Dylan, Charlotte, and Ling-Fei stood in the center of the cavern with their palms out.

Billy watched, hoping his jealousy wasn't too obvious. Even though he knew he would be getting his own pearl soon, he wished he had it at the same time as his friends.

And a small doubt had been planted in his head. What if he'd been wrong, and it wasn't the Lightning Pearl he'd seen? What if they couldn't find the fourth pearl? What if his friends all got special powers and Billy didn't? But it was more than that. Without the added protection of the pearl and its power, would he be able to survive in the Dragon Realm?

And there was something else. Something even bigger than his own survival. The dragons had made it clear they needed all four of the kids, with the pearls, to have a shot at defeating the Dragon of Death.

So Billy really, really hoped they could find that fourth pearl.

Tank came forward holding three shining pearls in his claws, all secured onto chain necklaces. "I'm a bit of a jeweler," he said, and then glared at everyone as if daring them to contradict him. "And this way you can wear the pearls and keep them close."

"Remember," said Xing. "The pearls awaken an inherent power within you. Something that you are already good at or comes to you naturally will be amplified. But if you are separated from the pearl, you will lose your power."

She took the chain holding the Jade Pearl from Tank in her teeth and dropped it over Ling-Fei's head. "Keep a closer eye on it this time," she said. Ling-Fei gripped it in her fist.

"I'll never lose it again," she said fiercely.

Tank presented Charlotte with the Gold Pearl.

"I've been saving this for a long time," he said. "The time is now. I hope you prove worthy of it."

"Of course I will," said Charlotte.

"Your confidence will serve you well in the Dragon Realm," said Tank, sounding proud.

"But do not let it be your downfall," warned Xing. "Listen to the others. Know your limitations."

"And for you, the Granite Pearl," Buttons said to Dylan, his voice low and sonorous, like a cello. "I do not know how your power will manifest, but I know it will be a great one. Do not doubt yourself."

Dylan nodded and held his head a little higher.

"Billy," Spark said gently, nudging him forward to his friends, "As you know, I don't have a pearl fo but I believe in you. You will find the fourth pear together we will defeat the Dragon of Death."

"How can you have so much faith in us?" ask "You've only just met us!"

"We can read a heart," said Spark. "And your hearts are loyal, strong, brave, and true."

"And now you have a little something ext side," said Xing, flying around them. "Tell m can you feel your powers?" She gazed intent Fei. "How do you feel?"

Ling-Fei blinked slowly, as if waking slumber. "There . . . are other living thing mountain," she said. "I can . . . hear them."

"Yes," said Tank. "There are fish in th lake."

"Can she hear the fish? Is it excepti that her power?" said Buttons excitedly.

"Be quiet!" hissed Xing. "Ling-Fei,

Ling-Fei lifted her head and peere was trying to pinpoint something. " exactly where the sun is, even thoug mountain. Isn't that strange?" She sou than usual.

"Have you always loved being i Ling-Fei nodded.

"It is too early to know for su

Everyone stared at him. "Are you all staring at me? I can sense it! That must be my power!"

"I . . . don't think that is a power," said Buttons.

Dylan slumped and opened his eyes. "Well, you *are* all staring at me. At least I was right about that." He looked at Buttons. "I feel the same as I did before," Dylan said. He tapped the Granite Pearl around his neck. "Maybe it's broken?"

"The pearls cannot break," said Tank.

"Ah. Then maybe *I'm* broken," said Dylan.

"Dylan, don't be ridiculous," said Billy. "We just don't know what your power is yet. It'll come."

"Sorry, Billy," said Dylan. "I should have insisted you get this pearl. It's wasted on me." He managed a small grin, but Billy could tell he was embarrassed.

"Don't worry, Dylan," said Ling-Fei kindly. "Billy's right. Your power will come."

"And your power is going to be the best one," said Billy. "I just know it."

"Thanks, Billy," said Dylan.

"Well, I don't know if there is a *best* power," said Charlotte. "But you'll definitely get a good one."

"Of course you'll get a good power," said Buttons.

"When you're finished wasting time reassuring the useless one that he isn't useless, might I suggest that you get back to your realm to find the fourth pearl?" said Xing.

Dylan stared at Xing. "Are you *sure* you have a heart like Ling-Fei's? Ling-Fei is the nicest person I've ever met, and you . . ."

115

"I'm what?" said Xing, moving her face very close to Dylan.

Dylan squirmed. "You are very intimidating, that's all."

"Stop tormenting my human," said Buttons, stepping between them. He looked at Dylan. "You'll find that Xing is like a melon—hard exterior protecting soft insides."

Xing poked Buttons in the belly with her claw. "You have soft insides *and* outsides," she said.

"Enough!" roared Tank. "Now that we have bonded and three of you have your pearls, there isn't any time to waste. The faster you can find the fourth pearl and get back to us, the better. We'll be waiting."

Billy cleared his throat. "And if we can't find it?" He wondered if they'd say that they would be fine with just the other three—that he shouldn't bother coming back.

"You will find it," said Spark. "We need all four of you to get back into our realm. We can't do it without you, Billy."

Even without a pearl of his own, Billy suddenly felt invincible.

"I won't let you down," he said. Then he looked at his friends. "I mean, *we* won't let you down."

CHAPTER 19
PORK BUNS AND PERSUASION

They left the mountain the way Billy had come in—through the hazy wall that was not a wall, up the tunnel, and out into the bright sunshine.

They stared at each other as if making sure they were all still there.

"Dragons," said Billy finally. "Actual, real-life dragons."

"I wonder . . ." said Charlotte. She went over to a fallen log and hoisted it easily over her shoulder. "It works!" she shouted. "The powers are real!"

Ling-Fei sat down on a rock and rubbed her temples. "I can sense so much . . . life all around me. All the plants. All the animals. Even the bugs. It's overwhelming."

Dylan's belly rumbled. Loudly. He looked at his watch. "It's almost lunch time!" He rubbed his stomach. "Can we get some food before we start our mission to save the world?"

"Yes, definitely," said Billy. "I'm starving. And as far as saving the world . . ." He paused. "Are you guys a little worried about what we've committed to?" Billy suddenly was. In the mountain, next to the dragons, he'd felt fearless, unstoppable. Now, back outside in the sunshine, back in the real world, he felt like just a kid. He couldn't believe that the fate of the entire world depended on him and his new friends.

"Of course I'm worried," said Ling-Fei, looking up. "But I know it's the right thing to do. The only thing."

Billy nodded.

"I'm terrified," said Dylan. "But I'm glad I'll have you all there with me."

Billy knew what Dylan meant. He'd always had friends back home, but they were school friends. Surf friends. Not the kind of friends he felt like he could truly be himself with. But with these three, even though they'd just met, he felt like he could trust them no matter what. They were all so different, but somehow, when they came together, they clicked and became something more. Billy didn't know if it was because of what they'd experienced and faced together or if it was deeper than that. If it was destiny.

"Exactly," said Charlotte. "You heard the dragons. Together we can win." She smiled at them. "I'm so happy I met y'all. Not just because we broke a magic curse together. But that definitely helps."

Back at camp, things looked normal. Some kids were playing on the grassy field, a few were lying in hammocks, and a couple were heading into the canteen; all of them enjoying a morning of free time.

In that moment, Billy felt the full weight of what could happen, and not just to him but to *everyone*. If they didn't stop the Dragon of Death, this would all be gone. Everything. His parents, his brother. The dragons had made it clear that the Dragon of Death would destroy the world as they knew it.

"It's weird, isn't it, that everything looks so normal?" asked Dylan as they went into the canteen. It was mostly empty, except for Shreya and Caroline, the camper from Denmark, in a far corner. "Nobody here knows there are dragons, like . . . *right there*. And that we are all in imminent danger."

"Do you think we should tell someone?" said Billy, the thought just occurring to him. "Maybe Old Gold? That way we don't need to break into his office. We could just ask for the pearl."

"I don't know," said Charlotte. "He wouldn't believe us."

"He might," said Billy. "He's the one who told us about the legend in the first place."

"Even if he did believe us, he wouldn't let us go back to the mountain," said Ling-Fei as they approached the steamer and grabbed as many stuffed buns as they could carry. "He'd want to protect us. I know that. And . . . we can't let the dragons down. You heard them. It has to be us."

"I guess you know Old Gold better than any of us," said Billy.

They took their food to a table at the back of the canteen. Billy was ravenous, and the buns were delicious. They were fluffy and hot and filled with tangy sweet meat.

"These are good," Dylan said, with his mouth full. "What's in them?"

"Char-siu," said Ling-Fei. "It's a kind of barbequed pork."

"I like it," said Dylan, reaching for another bun. They chewed in silence for a few moments, letting the buns revive them. They were so focused on eating they didn't notice Old Gold walk up to their table, JJ right behind him.

"Good afternoon," said Old Gold.

"Good afternoon," they chorused.

"Do you mind if we join you?" he said.

There was only one answer to that.

"Of course not," said Charlotte graciously. "Would you like a bun?"

"I've already eaten, actually. I just wanted to have a little chat," said Old Gold, settling into a chair next to Billy. JJ stayed standing, his arms folded.

"JJ said he saw something quite interesting this morning. Or rather, what he didn't see. Apparently, he couldn't find any sign of you all over camp," said Old Gold. "I know you had free time, but it is strange for you four to be so hard to find."

Billy bristled. Why had JJ been looking for them? He glanced over at Dylan to roll his eyes, but Dylan was staring directly at JJ and Old Gold with a strange expression on his face.

Ling-Fei's eyes grew enormous. "Yeye, we can explain," she started, her voice beginning to rise in panic, before Dylan interrupted smoothly.

"JJ," he said with a grin, "that is so kind of you to be looking out for us. But you know we were studying Chinese in our cabins. Remember?"

JJ stared back at Dylan and then blinked. "Oh, yeah," he said slowly. "I guess I forgot."

"You were all studying?" asked Old Gold, sounding much more skeptical.

"We were," said Dylan, turning his gaze on Old Gold. "We wanted to make up for our abysmal performance in the scavenger hunt."

Old Gold nodded. "Of course you were," he said.

"Thank you for checking on us," Dylan went on. "Oh, and one more thing . . ."

It suddenly hit Billy. Whatever was going on here had something to do with Dylan's power. It had to.

"Yes?" said Old Gold, looking a bit dazed.

Dylan stared directly into Old Gold's eyes. "Tonight, you should leave your office door unlocked. Everyone here at camp is very trustworthy."

"Leave my office door unlocked?" repeated Old Gold.

"Yes," said Dylan. "Unlocked." Then he cleared his throat. "Was there anything else you wanted to ask us, Old Gold?"

Old Gold shook his head, as if he were clearing it.

"Glad to see you four getting along so well," he said. "Come along, JJ. I need your help organizing my files." He shuffled away.

JJ stared at the table. "I don't know what is happening, but something weird is going on with you guys," he said.

"I don't know what you're talking about," said Dylan, taking a big bite of pork bun.

As soon as JJ had left the canteen, Dylan turned to the others with a grin.

"I think I figured out my power."

"Lying?" said Charlotte, eyebrows raised.

"How insulting," said Dylan. "Not lying. *Persuading*."

"Whatever it was, it was impressive," said Billy. "I can't believe you got Old Gold to leave his door unlocked."

"He hasn't done it yet," said Dylan. "But I decided it was worth a shot. It was the strangest thing; when I saw them, I knew we were going to be in trouble, and I realized that if I started talking, well, they would believe me."

"It makes sense," said Ling-Fei. "You tell good stories. Charm would come naturally to you."

"It's an awesome power," said Billy. "I wonder if it works on dragons."

"I hope so," said Dylan. "I'm just glad it worked on Old Gold and JJ."

"So am I," said Charlotte. "But Dylan? If you ever try that on me, I will use my own power to pound you into the ground. Got it?"

Dylan gulped. "Got it."

CHAPTER 20
THE LIGHTNING PEARL

They made a plan to meet at midnight outside Old Gold's office.

"What if Old Gold doesn't leave his door unlocked after all?" said Dylan as they left the canteen.

"He *will*," said Charlotte.

"And if he doesn't, we'll have to break in the old-fashioned way," said Billy. "Through a window or something."

"Or I can bust the door down," said Charlotte.

"I think we should avoid that if possible," said Ling-Fei. She paused. "And I think we should leave Old Gold a note. So he doesn't worry."

"That's a good idea," said Dylan. He swallowed. "I want to write a note for my family, too. Just in case . . . we don't come back."

They all looked at each other, suddenly aware that not returning home was a very real possibility.

Charlotte broke the silence. "Well, aren't you a bunch of pessimistic possums?" she said, tossing her hair. "Obviously we're coming back. Just after we defeat the Dragon of Death and save the world. Easy-peasy."

It was unclear if she was kidding or not. Charlotte sighed. "But if y'all are leaving notes for your families, I'll do the same. Just so my daddy doesn't panic when the camp calls to say we've run off."

"Ling-Fei," said Billy slowly. "You can't tell Old Gold in the note where we've gone or what we're doing."

"I won't," she said. "I'll just say we've gone . . ."

". . . on an adventure," said Charlotte firmly. "And we'll be back soon."

Back in his cabin, Billy sat down at his small desk. Dylan sat next to him and passed him a piece of paper.

"I'm not exactly sure what to write," Dylan admitted, pushing his glasses up on his nose. "We can't explain much, can we?"

Billy shook his head. "I guess not."

He looked down at his paper and started writing. *Dear Mom, Dad, and Eddie.*

He paused. His stomach was starting to hurt. What if he never saw his parents again? Or his brother? He couldn't imagine it.

"Hey, Dylan," he said quietly.

Dylan looked up. "Yeah?"

"Are you scared?"

Dylan laughed a little. "Petrified," he said. "But . . . I still think we should go. And what are our other options?

Pretend we never discovered *dragons*? *Talking dragons?* Just go back to life like normal even though we know that the Dragon of Death is coming?"

Billy nodded. "You're right," he said. "I just hope we can go home at the end of it all."

"Me, too," said Dylan. "But Billy?"

"What?"

"I really do think everything will be okay. I've got to think that, otherwise I'd never be able to go into something like this. And we'll all be together. With dragons!"

"You're right," said Billy. He took a deep breath and thought about Spark. Deep inside himself, he could have sworn he felt an answering tug, like an invisible tether running back to the mountain—back to Spark. It made him feel calm and strong.

He looked back at his paper. He knew what to say.

"Everything at camp is great. Mom and Dad, you were right. I'm glad I came. I just wanted to tell you guys that I love you. And I hope I can make you proud."

The rest of the day passed in a blur.

They had dinner with the other campers, avoiding Old Gold and JJ. After, when they were all sitting by the campfire, Ling-Fei asked Old Gold to retell the legend of Dragon Mountain.

And then, despite all the excitement, Billy slept until his alarm went off at midnight. He sat bolt upright. It was time.

The door to Old Gold's office was unlocked.

Dylan heaved a huge sigh of relief. "I guess my power really does work," he said, his hand on the pearl around his neck.

"Stop congratulating yourself and get looking for the pearl," said Charlotte, slipping inside the office.

Without the moon and stars overhead, darkness hung heavy in the office, and Billy let his eyes adjust, trying to make out the shapes.

Charlotte turned on a flashlight. "Thought this might be useful," she said.

"Careful," said Dylan, eyeing the windows. "We don't want anyone to see we're in here."

Charlotte nodded and pointed the light down toward the ground.

"Where do we start?" said Dylan. "Billy, do you remember where anything was?"

Billy shook his head, feeling a bit useless. "It was really rainy," he said. "All I saw was the light flashing and the blue glow."

"Ah. A blue glow," said Dylan, glancing doubtfully around the decidedly normal-looking office.

"Wait," said Ling-Fei. "I can sense something." She went to a cupboard and opened it, her hands trembling. Then she gasped.

"What is it?" asked Billy. "Have you found the pearl?" He desperately hoped she had. He had been so sure the Lightning Pearl was here. He didn't want to let the dragons down, and he didn't want to be the only one without a pearl. He'd thought it would be obvious, but if the pearl *was* here, he couldn't see it.

Ling-Fei held out her hands. In them were what looked like pieces of oblong ivory.

"These are oracle bones," breathed Ling-Fei.

"What's an oracle bone?" asked Dylan, leaving the desk drawer he was rummaging through to inspect Ling-Fei's discovery.

"They're ancient fortune-telling devices," said Ling-Fei, turning the bones over in her hand. "I knew Old Gold collected ancient artifacts, but these . . . these are priceless and incredibly rare."

"As rare as a magic pearl?" said Billy with a wry grin.

"No, but they are very rare. And useful. I think we should show these to the dragons," said Ling-Fei, putting one in her pocket.

"Ling-Fei, aren't bones, by their very nature, a bit . . . dead?" asked Dylan.

"What do you mean?" said Ling-Fei.

"Doesn't your power help you sense . . . *living* things? Isn't it strange that you found the bones?"

Ling-Fei nodded slowly. "That's what I thought." She pulled out the oracle bone again. "But this is definitely calling to me. And it feels . . . alive."

They all stared at the ivory bone, as if waiting for it to jump up in the air. A shiver ran down Billy's spine.

"Maybe you can sense magic, too, the way Xing can," said Charlotte to Ling-Fei. "If that is the case, maybe you could try to sense the Lightning Pearl."

"Good idea, Charlotte," said Billy, even though he wished that he was the one who could sense it.

Ling-Fei closed her eyes and focused. Then her eyes

flew open, and she pointed to the top of a bookshelf. "There. There's something there."

Billy looked up and saw a wink of flashing blue light. "I see something!" he said. He clambered up the bookshelf as if it were a ladder. He could see the pearl now. It glowed blue, and inside it, tiny bolts of lightning danced around, as if trying to escape.

"A storm trapped in a pearl," Billy said in wonder as he reached out and grabbed it. The pearl sparked in his hands, sending small jolts of electricity up his arms. "Whoa."

"Do you have it?" said Charlotte from below.

Billy turned to hop down from the bookshelf, but what started as a jump turned into a backflip. He landed on two feet, the pearl still clutched in his hand.

His friends stared at him.

"Have you . . . always been able to do that?" said Dylan.

Billy shook his head and then grinned. "I think my power has been activated."

CHAPTER 21
SUIT UP

This time, the walk back to the mountain felt different. Purposeful. It was dark outside, but the Lightning Pearl lit up enough to show the path. They had decided to go straight to the mountain instead of waiting until morning. The sooner they returned to their dragons, the better. They marched in silence, excitement radiating off them like steam from a hot bowl of soup.

They found the dragons in the main cavern. As soon as Billy saw Spark, he was filled with that same sense of strength and calm he'd had when he thought about her earlier. But now it was magnified. He felt invincible.

"You came back," said Tank.

"Of course we did," said Charlotte.

"Humans are fickle creatures," said Xing. But she was smiling. "I'm hoping you succeeded in what we asked of you."

"We found the Lightning Pearl," said Billy, reaching into his pocket and holding it out.

"And?" said Spark, giving Billy her sharp-toothed smile.

Billy leaped into the air and did two somersaults. "I think my power has something to do with balance and agility," he said, landing on silent feet.

"My power showed itself, too!" said Dylan, telling them what had happened with Old Gold.

Buttons applauded. "A delightful power! And so useful, too."

"Intriguing, that a human would have a pearl and oracle bones," said Xing, inspecting the oracle bone that Ling-Fei had brought back. "This one is about us, the return of the dragons."

"Do you think Old Gold has read it?" asked Ling-Fei.

"Humans rarely know how to read them properly. Even if he did, he wouldn't know what it meant," said Xing dismissively.

"And now . . . now do we go into the Dragon Realm?" asked Billy.

Tank appraised them. "We will go soon. When we get there, the first thing we should do is find our old clan, alongside whom we battled the Dragon of Death and her nox-wings. Our old friend Dimitrius will have been in charge. And then we will find out why the Dragon of Death is growing in strength, even back in time when she should be unable to do anything."

"It has to be something to do with those wretched

nox-wings," sniffed Buttons. "Odious creatures, really. Would do anything for a bit of ill-begotten power."

"Before we go, there's one more thing," said Xing. "We need to get you properly clothed." She made a derisive sound. "Humans, with their soft skin and weak bones. Such a liability."

"I quite like my skin," said Dylan.

"Then you probably want to keep it on your body," said Xing. "Now come with me!"

They followed Xing down the corridor to her hoard. She dove in, sniffing around, and then pushed out a jeweled trunk. She popped it open with her nose. Shining fabric spilled out.

"Is that . . . living fabric?" asked Ling-Fei, moving closer. "I can sense it."

"It's magic, not living," said Xing. "But your power seems to already be growing." She shouted, "Spark! I need your help."

Spark flew in on silent wings.

"Use your . . . electricity thing," said Xing.

"These bolts of fabric are incredibly rare and very valuable," Spark explained. "They will be able to protect you from almost anything." She smiled. "It's the closest thing to dragon skin we can give you."

"You," said Xing, pointing her snout at Dylan. "We'll start with you. Come here."

A sheet of metallic green fabric rose up from the trunk, as if on its own accord, and swept over Dylan, covering him completely.

Xing focused on Dylan. Her eyes glowed, and a light

emanated from them. Spark made a low buzzing sound, and bolts of electricity zapped from her wings toward Dylan. He giggled as one hit him.

"That tickles," he said, squirming.

"Hold still," said Xing.

Billy stared in amazement as the fabric morphed around Dylan's body, shaping itself to his figure. The neck hole stretched around his head, revealing Dylan's shocked face. Then the two dragons exhaled. Dylan stood in front of them, wearing a full body suit of metallic green.

"You look like a superhero!" said Ling-Fei.

"I feel like a superhero!" said Dylan, stretching in it. He looked up at Xing and Spark. "Thank you!"

Xing snorted. "Thanks are not required," she said. "We're taking necessary precautions." She looked over at Billy, Charlotte, and Ling-Fei. "Who's next?"

Charlotte leapt forward. "Can mine have a skirt on it? You know, just to be fashionable? Ooh, and pockets?"

Xing stared at Charlotte a long moment and then grinned, showing her diamond teeth. "I understand wanting a bit of aesthetic appeal," she said.

"And pockets are very useful," said Charlotte.

After Xing and Spark were done with Charlotte's suit, it looked almost like Dylan's, but in bright red and gold to match Tank's scales and with a skirt over the pants. And pockets. Charlotte twirled in delight, hands stuck deep in her pockets, and the skirt flared out.

Ling-Fei's suit was shimmering silver and gold, with a high collar and a hood draped down her back. "I gave you pockets, too," said Xing with a wink.

"Now it's your turn," Spark said to Billy.

Billy let himself be encased in blue shimmering fabric. It pinched a bit, and he felt small shocks as Spark's electric power morphed the material around him. When his head emerged out of the top, he gasped.

His suit ran from his ankles to his wrists, and even though it was snug, he could still move freely in it. It was like the most amazing wetsuit he had ever dreamed of. A *magical* wetsuit.

"We look amazing!" cried Charlotte. "I feel ready for anything."

"Well, that's good," said Spark. "Because we need to be ready for anything."

The joyful mood that had filled the cavern while they were being fitted for their suits evaporated.

"We'll do everything we can to protect you, but we can't deny how dangerous it will be," said Spark.

"We know," said Billy.

Before yesterday he hadn't even known dragons existed. And now he knew there was an entire world of them. A world at war. A world at war that needed their help.

CHAPTER 22
THE KEEPER OF THE CURSE

"We're ready," said Billy, clenching his fists at his side. Adrenaline coursed through him.

"Before we go, you must get some rest," said Tank.

"I don't think I can sleep," said Billy. "I'm way too pumped up."

"And no offense, but the rock floor doesn't look very comfortable," said Dylan.

"There will be far fewer comforts ahead," said Xing.

"I will sing you to sleep," announced Buttons.

"That sounds nice," said Ling-Fei, lying down.

"What?" asked Charlotte, incredulous.

"Lie down," said Spark. "You'll see."

Billy, Charlotte, and Dylan joined Ling-Fei on the hard stone ground.

This won't work, Billy thought. Then Buttons let

out a low hum that sounded like a cello, and before Billy could think anything else, he was fast asleep.

Billy woke to the smell of grilled fish. He blinked, trying to make sense of his surroundings. Yes, he was still in a cavern with dragons. Yes, his friends were right next to him.

And so was a giant grilled fish. It was bigger than he was.

"Where did that come from?" he asked, running his hand through his hair.

"How do you think we survived all this time? There's an underground lake in this mountain. We've been eating fish for years," said Buttons.

"I'm so sick of eating fish," added Xing. "I can't wait to get back home."

"Enough talking," said Tank. "Eat quickly. Spark has had another vision. The Dragon of Death is closer than ever. We need to hurry."

And then it was time.

"This is your chance to turn back," said Spark. "Once we enter our realm, you will be in greater danger than you have ever experienced."

Billy looked at his friends. At their dragons. And he knew that no matter what lay ahead of them, he was ready to face it. His friends nodded back at him, and he realized they felt the same.

"We're ready," he said.

"Good," said Tank. "Follow us."

The dragons led them down a long, dark corridor

until they reached a wall of dark purple fog. As they approached, Billy saw lightning flash from within it. He swallowed and shifted closer to Spark.

"Wait!" said Tank, motioning for the group to stop.

The kids came to a halt and stared at the swirling wall of fog.

"Is *this* the entrance to the Dragon Realm?" Dylan asked.

"It is," said Xing, narrowing her eyes. "Though the dark magic cast by the Dragon of Death is still sealing the entrance."

"Does that mean what I think it means?" Buttons said, exchanging a look with the other dragons.

"Let us find out," said Xing. She lowered her head and plucked a scale from her own body with her teeth. With a flick of her neck, she tossed the silver scale toward the wall.

A bolt of light shot out and struck the scale in midair. Billy heard a soft *pop* as the scale disintegrated into a puff of ash.

"*What* was that?" asked Dylan, taking a few steps backward.

"Children," said Tank, the scar across his face turning a deep crimson red as he spoke. "I am afraid you will be tested sooner than we would have wished. The curse will not let us dragons get any closer. The four of you will have to pass through this fog to reopen the entrance to the Dragon Realm. Your four hearts together opened the path to the Human Realm, and it will have to be you four again to open the entrance to the Dragon Realm."

Billy felt light-headed, and he took a deep breath to calm himself. This was it. This might be the last thing that he ever did. He thought about his life at home, his life before dragons. And he realized that even if this *was* the end, it would be worth it. To get a chance to experience magic in the world. To be a part of something epic.

"Whoa, whoa, whoa," said Dylan holding up his hands. "You're telling me that we have to walk through this lightning-shooting wall by ourselves? Did you *see* what it did to that scale? Surely there's another way? A back entrance we could use that isn't cursed quite as much as this one? One that shoots, I don't know, water balloons instead of lightning?"

Billy turned to Dylan and gripped him by the shoulders. "Dylan, you know the answers to these questions. It has to be us. We can do this. We are doing this."

"And we'll have each other," said Ling-Fei, coming closer.

"Yeah," added Charlotte. "And if anything tries to get us, I'll pummel it with my fists." She shook her clenched fist in the air for emphasis.

Dylan let out a small laugh and managed to smile at his friends. "All right, then," he said, looking at their dragons.

Xing cleared her throat. "Whenever you're ready, warriors."

"We believe in you," added Buttons.

Everyone grew silent as the children approached the wall that wasn't a wall. Billy steeled his nerves. He took a big step toward it, waiting to see if he'd be zapped by the lightning. He counted to three. Nothing happened. He looked at Charlotte, Dylan, and Ling-Fei and gave them an encouraging nod. They could do this. He took another step forward, more sure of himself this time, and then another. The others followed until they were standing so close to the wall that the swirling purple fog licked at their faces. Billy reached his hands out on either side of him. "Are we ready?"

"Ready," said Charlotte.

"Ready," said Ling-Fei.

"Let's do this," said Dylan.

They joined hands and stepped into the fog together, leaving their dragons behind.

Walking through the fog felt no different than walking through a thick morning mist. They emerged into another dark cavern, one with a faint purple glow. As Billy's eyes adjusted, he saw thin purple veins climbing the walls like ivy, twitching as if blood coursed through them. Dark clouds carpeted the floor.

"What do we do now?" whispered Dylan.

Billy scanned their surroundings. He couldn't see any other passages—just the single, large cavern. They were trapped.

Before Billy had time to respond, a shape rose out of the storm, and purple lightning flashed across the cavern.

Something resembling a tiger emerged, its body made of the same thick black fog and laced with bright purple veins that flowed to a massive heart beating in the center of its chest. It studied the four children and seemed to smile. "Well, well, well. We meet again, tiny humans. I see you've dressed for the occasion this time." It threw its head back and let out a bark of laughter that sounded like a thunder strike.

The children pulled closer together. Billy stared hard at the purple tiger. There was something familiar about it. "Are you the tiger that chased us?"

"Very good!" exclaimed the tiger. "Why, yes, indeed. It is me! They say a tiger never changes its stripes, yet here I am. Orange yesterday and purple today. You can call me Victor. I picked the name myself. Oh, what a joy that was—so many options! Now, if you'd come last week, you would have had to call me Diana. So boring, being tied to just one name, don't you think? I like to switch it up. Those hopeless dragons of yours, on the other hand, really take the whole naming thing seriously, but that's another conversation."

The tiger blew out a cloud of smoke that churned around in the air until it formed a huge floating throne. Then it hopped up into the chair before placing a crown made of lightning on its head.

"I think we were zapped by lightning and now we're dead," said Dylan, his eyes gigantic. "This can't be happening."

"Do you want me to pinch you again?" said Charlotte. "Focus! Now is not the time to fall apart!"

"It's strange," said Ling-Fei, addressing the tiger. "I sense you are both alive and . . . not alive. How can this be?"

"Clever girl," said the tiger. "I am the Keeper of the Curse." His voice deepened and boomed,

"Four dragons trapped far from view
Waiting for four hearts loyal, strong, brave, and true.
Four hearts to match their own
To open this mountain made of stone."

The tiger returned to its normal voice. "As you see, there's nothing in the curse about you four going into the Dragon Realm. Just *opening* the mountain."

"Opening the mountain on both sides surely," said Billy.

"It doesn't specify that. And as the Keeper of the Curse, I'm the one who decides what means what. I didn't fry you alive when you came through the wall as I would have done to your four dragons, which was very kind of me, you must agree. Now the only way to get through into the other realm is to beat me, and I'm afraid four children against an all-mighty tiger gifted with the powers of the Great One have no chance." The tiger licked its lips.

Billy felt his lungs constrict. *Stay calm*, he told himself. He felt a tug on the thread that connected him to Spark. She was telling him to stay calm, too.

Then he remembered their powers. "Dylan," he whispered. "Do the thing. Your thing!"

Dylan nodded and raised his voice. "What an honor it is to meet you properly, Victor. A wonderful place you have here. I love what you've done with the lighting, really sets the mood. Now, I'm sure this is all just one big misunderstanding. Perhaps you could bend the rules just this once and let us through to the Dragon Realm?"

The tiger let out another deep, cackling roar. "Oh, what a funny boy you are! Your ignorance and tenacity are impressive in equal measure. Your pitiful persuasions and charms won't work on me. But that was a half-decent try. You've come a long way since we last met. Quite the runner, you were."

Billy sensed a change in the air just before the tiger unhinged its jaw and released a tidal wave of electricity toward them. "Watch out!" he shouted, jerking his friends to the side before the wave reached them. "We're going to have to fight." An idea struck Billy. "I'll do my best to distract the tiger, and you guys figure out where its weaknesses are." He felt braver than he ever had, and he wasn't sure if it was because of his new powers or because he was with his friends, but in that moment, he wasn't afraid at all.

He stood steady before the tiger. "Is that all you have?" Billy shouted. "That's pathetic! Any average human could have dodged that blast. Why don't you try to get me . . . if you can?" He dropped Charlotte's hand and raced along the wall of the cavern, hoping the tiger would focus all its attention on him. He felt reckless and exhilarated but also strangely confident. He believed in his friends and that together they could defeat the tiger. He believed in himself.

"Oh, you are even more dim-witted than your long-legged friend!" said the tiger. "But you do seem faster, I'll give you that." Victor turned to Billy and let out another torrent of electricity. Billy leaped high into the air, just dodging the tiger's attack. He kicked off the wall and shot off in another direction. The tiger let out a disgruntled roar and spit more lightning at Billy.

Billy found he could sense the streams of lightning coming at him before the tiger shot them out, and he dodged the attacks with ease, flipping off the walls and bending in every direction. As Billy darted around the cavern, he looked back toward his friends. He could only keep this up for so long. The boldness and confidence he'd had before started to waver, and a tendril of fear crept in. He stumbled, and one of the tiger's lightning bolts came dangerously close to his face. He yelped and dove in the other direction.

"We have to do something before he gets fried alive!" he heard Dylan shout to Charlotte and Ling-Fei.

"Its heart!" Ling-Fei suddenly blurted, hope in her voice. "I don't know how I can tell, but we have to get to its heart." Her voice sounded very far away to Billy, who didn't dare take his eyes off the tiger even for a second. He wasn't sure he had heard Ling-Fei right. Getting to the tiger's heart sounded like an impossible task.

All Billy knew was he was getting tired and the tiger wasn't. If anything, it was starting to feel like the tiger was toying with him the way a cat would play with a mouse.

"Hurry," Billy croaked out as he dodged another lightning strike just in time.

And then his friends crept closer. Billy used his last burst of strength to run up the wall to keep distracting the tiger.

As he glanced below, he saw Charlotte dash straight toward the tiger, who was still focused on Billy, and punch her hand through its back, ripping out its beating purple heart.

Billy dropped down from the wall as the tiger collapsed with a roar. "What? How can this be? Defeated by tiny humans," the tiger choked out, turning its gaze toward each of the children. "You may have won this battle, but you will never stop the Great One!"

The heart in Charlotte's hand disappeared, and the tiger gave out a final cry as it shimmered into nothingness.

CHAPTER 23
THE OTHER SIDE OF THE MOUNTAIN

"We did it!" yelled Ling-Fei. "Billy, you were amazing! And Charlotte, that was . . . wild!"

"What a punch," said Dylan, who looked shell-shocked.

Charlotte grinned. "I told you I would pummel anything that tried to get us with my fists."

"We survived! We broke the curse!" said Billy. He felt invincible. If they could defeat a magic tiger and break an evil curse on their own, they would be unstoppable with their dragons. The glow from the purple veins on the walls was fading quickly, and soon it was so dark Billy couldn't see his own hands. He pulled his friends closer as the ground began to shake.

"I think the mountain is opening into the Dragon Realm!" said Charlotte.

Billy looked up to see one side of the cavern slowly cracking open until it looked like a giant doorway, filling the entire cavern with sunlight. It was so bright, Billy shielded his eyes, unable to see past the light-filled entrance. He turned back around, blinking, and saw the dragons emerge from the wall of fog.

"Spark!" he cried.

"You did it!" thundered Tank. "You broke the curse!"

"I knew you would," said Spark.

"You have done very well for such small humans," said Xing. She nuzzled Ling-Fei with her snout.

"We're going home!" cried Buttons. He turned toward the sunlit entrance and rolled around on the cavern floor. "Sunshine! Air! I'd almost forgotten how wonderful it is."

"Stop acting like a common lizard," snapped Xing. "Get off the ground. I'm eager to see our home, and you can roll around on the ground as much as you like then."

"Fine, fine," said Buttons. But he was smiling widely as he stood and lifted his face to the sun like a giant sunflower.

"Before we reenter our realm, we should be ready to fly," said Tank. "Quickly, now."

"The bond will help us to fly as one and keep you secure on our backs," said Spark as she kneeled low enough for Billy to climb on.

Billy climbed up on Spark's back, his hands still trembling with the adrenaline of the battle with the tiger and in anticipation of riding a dragon.

"Hold on," Spark said, straightening up to her full height. He was riding a *dragon*. It was like all his childhood dreams had come true. They hadn't even taken flight yet, and it was already amazing. Billy's face split into a wide, irrepressible grin. He hoped he would remember this exact moment forever.

Billy looked over at each of his friends astride their dragons. Dylan gave him a salute from the back of Buttons. Charlotte looked like an avenging warrior queen on Tank's back. Ling-Fei sat proudly on Xing, like she'd been riding dragons all her life.

They were no longer the children who had arrived at summer camp.

They were champions, ready for anything.

"Onward," roared Tank.

The dragons strode forward, the children on their backs, and they emerged from the cavern and into the Dragon Realm.

Billy gazed out at the new world in front of him. In a dusty red sky, three full moons sat above an oval sun. Even in the harsh daylight, millions of stars winked at them. Islands hovered in the air like giant clouds, exposed roots dangling beneath as if they'd been plucked from the earth. Below the plateau they stood on, rivers flowed between the mountains like serpents.

Everything in sight looked as if it had been scorched by fire. Despite the flowing rivers, there was almost no plant life except for one type of tree with green leaves and pink flowers that dotted the landscape.

Spark slowly approached the edge of the plateau. "Things look far worse than I expected," she said, her eyes narrow. "This land was lush and dotted with fruit when we left the Dragon Realm over a hundred years ago."

Billy felt a shiver run down his spine. He didn't know what he had been expecting, but it wasn't this. Were they really the ones to stop whatever caused all of this devastation? His elation at defeating the tiger and riding Spark faded as he realized the magnitude of what he and his friends were taking on—and how unprepared the dragons suddenly seemed to be. He couldn't let himself go down that train of thought; otherwise he'd run straight back home.

"Hey, look! At least there's still fruit growing here," said Dylan, distracting Billy from his thoughts. Dylan hopped off of Buttons's back and plucked a round fuzzy fruit from a nearby tree. Then he held it farther away from him and looked up nervously. "This isn't going to explode or anything, is it?"

"It looks like a peach," said Charlotte, coming up behind him. "I should know, being from the peach state and all. I doubt it will explode."

Dylan shrugged. "I also doubted the existence of dragons, and here we are. Besides, surely there aren't things as normal as peaches in the Dragon Realm?"

"I like how you think, Dylan," said Buttons. "You are right that things in our realm are not always what they seem. These fruits are one of those things. You see, peaches are very special in the Dragon Realm. Once every few thousand years, a peach will grow that grants the one who eats it *immortality*."

Dylan eyed the ripe peach in his hand. "You mean, one of these could make me *immortal*?"

Buttons gave Dylan a smile. "Well, it could," he said

as he reached out his paw and slapped it from Dylan's hand. The peach popped up into the air and fell right into Buttons's open mouth. "Or it could be just another ordinary peach. Hard to tell."

"*Cool*," said Dylan, plucking more peaches from the branches and taking a bite from each one. "I love peaches. Maybe one of these is a peach of immortality!"

"Enough," said Tank, his voice harsh. "We must focus."

"Sorry," said Dylan, his face red and his mouth still full. He plucked a few more peaches from the tree and stuffed them into his bag before getting on Buttons's back again.

"There will be plenty of time for peaches," said Buttons. "The trees grow everywhere in the Dragon Realm. And unlike the peach trees in your realm, these ones are almost indestructible."

"It must be why they are the only things that have survived . . . whatever happened here," said Spark, her voice serious. "The Dragon of Death's followers, the Noxious, must be using dark magic to bring their leader back. It would explain why everything we see is dead or dying."

"I fear you are right," said Xing. "A very dark magic has taken over our land. The nox-wings must have grown more powerful in our absence. I worry that our clan might be in danger."

"What exactly is dark magic?" asked Ling-Fei.

Spark turned to face the children. "Everything in our universe is made of energy. Each of us standing here on this plateau. The plants in your forests, the fish in your seas. The moon and the stars you see in the sky. Everything. It is this energy that makes each of us special. It makes us who we are. It is the source of your inner powers, the source of your inspiration." Spark gazed back toward the scorched earth below. "It is a sacred and powerful energy, and it can be taken to create a dark and powerful magic."

A chill passed through Billy as he imagined what it would be like to have his energy taken from him. He felt as if he were being hollowed out from the inside. He tried to gasp for air, but nothing came.

"Billy," said Spark, interrupting his thoughts. She nuzzled Billy gently on the cheek, and Billy turned to look at her.

She didn't speak, but Billy heard Spark's voice in his head. *Do not fear, Billy.*

The chill loosened its grip. He could feel Spark's strength and determination through their bond, and he felt comforted. He smiled at her. *How am I hearing your voice?* he thought.

Spark returned his smile, and Billy heard her voice in his head again. *Every bond is unique, and it seems that we share an inner voice. When we are close, we can share our thoughts. I sensed it when we first bonded, but here in the Dragon Realm, our connection is stronger.*

I'm glad we're in this together, Billy thought back, filled with relief that no matter what happened, he'd have his dragon by his side.

"Billy," said Charlotte, concern on her face. "Are you okay?"

"I think so," Billy replied. "This is all a bit over-whelming, you know?"

Charlotte nodded.

"The Dragon of Death and the Noxious are strong, and this is a whole new world for you. It makes sense that you feel uncertain," said Spark. "But feel comfort in knowing that we are stronger. We have our bonds, and we have the pearls—we will win this fight."

"Spark is right," said Tank. "We are strong. Our bonds will overpower the evil that has consumed this land. We will defeat the Noxious. Our clan's lair is about a day's journey away. Let us fly there and tell Dimitrius and the others that we have returned."

Tank dashed to the edge of the plateau and dove out of sight. Xing and Buttons followed, Dylan shouting as they did. Billy swallowed. This was it. This was his first time flying. *Hold on, Billy*, Spark thought, and she took off into the air. Wind whipped through Billy's hair, and adrenaline pumped through his veins. He had never felt more alive.

They flew for hours, staying in a tight formation. Billy scanned the land as they traveled, his muscles tense and his eyes alert. Whatever had caused so much widespread destruction had to be incredibly strong. He knew how serious the situation was, and he wanted to prove the dragons right—that he, Dylan, Charlotte, and Ling-Fei were the ones to save both their worlds. Every now and then, pebbles and dirt rained down from the underside of an island floating above them. The landscape beneath them stayed the same, with rivers flowing through ravaged desert ravines and tufts of peach trees dotting the land.

As they flew, Billy practiced communicating with Spark using only his thoughts, sharing some openly and keeping others to himself. He found that flying with Spark was a joint effort. He felt the bond as if it were part of him, and through it, he could feel the movements of Spark's wings as if they were his own. The closest feeling he'd ever had to it was when he was surfing, flying on the waves. But this, *real* flying, this was so much better.

As the sun started to set and darkness crept up on them, the three full moons climbed high in the sky among millions of twinkling stars that seemed to wander like fireflies. It was the most beautiful sky Billy had ever seen. As the group flew around a sharp river bend, Tank called out, "We're almost there. Everyone stay alert."

Ahead Billy saw a large mountain, almost as large as Dragon Mountain. They flew toward the side of it and swooped into the mouth of a cave that seemed to appear from nowhere.

"It shouldn't be so quiet," said Spark, concern in her voice.

When his eyes had adjusted, the first thing Billy spotted was what looked to be a large hoard of dragon treasure. He gasped when he saw what it really was.

Bones. Hundreds and hundreds of bones. Billy had never seen dragon bones before, but he suspected that these bones belonged to the dragons that they had come to find. He was suddenly filled with a deep sense of anguish, and he knew for sure that his suspicions were right.

Xing let out a screaming roar that echoed through the cavern.

"We are too late," said Tank.

"How . . . ?" cried Buttons.

Xing flew around and around the pile of bones, her whole body trembling.

"I had no idea," whispered Spark.

Billy felt an ache in his heart, and tears pooled in his eyes. He could feel Spark's loss and her agony. "I'm sorry," he said, resting his hand on her side.

Spark hung her head. "This cannot be. I didn't see any of this in my visions."

"Maybe we should get out of here before whatever did this . . . comes back," said Dylan anxiously, looking around.

"We can't give up!" cried Charlotte. "If anything, this means we have to keep going. Right, Tank?"

"Charlotte is right," said Tank. "We must find the nox-wings. And find out who is still alive. There must be survivors . . . somewhere." He turned his gaze to Xing. "Can you sense any magic nearby?"

Xing closed her eyes, and her body thrummed. The others waited in silence as Xing focused her energy. A short moment passed before her eyes shot open. "There is a concentration of dark magic just north of here." She flew out of the cave with Ling-Fei and up toward the sky. "Follow me!" she yelled to the others, who rushed to join her.

"Look, there!" cried Xing.

A red dome rose out of the horizon, its unnaturalness a stark contrast to the mountains stretching toward the sky. The dome was semitransparent, with eight plumes of smoke rising from within it.

"What is that?" asked Billy. "It looks big enough to cover my whole neighborhood back home!" Something about the dome made the hairs on the back of his neck stand up. It looked like it shouldn't be there.

"I do not know. It is new, and it reeks of dark magic," said Xing, wrinkling her snout. "It must be where the Noxious are."

"Then that is where we must go," said Spark.

CHAPTER 24
A SURPRISING REUNION

Even from a distance the red dome looked ominous. The group landed on a mountain a few miles away to see if they could figure out what was happening. For the first time since entering the Dragon Realm, Billy saw plants that weren't peach trees. A dense forest of purple and black plant life surrounded the red dome.

"Why have those plants around the red dome survived?" asked Dylan. "Is that what all of the Dragon Realm used to look like?"

Spark shook her head. "Those horrific plants must be the by-products of the dark magic being used by the Noxious. Whatever they are doing beneath that dome, it is draining the rest of the Dragon Realm of its life and leaving bare what was once lush." She looked at the other dragons. "This is worse than what I have seen in my visions and worse than what we suspected might have happened. This desolation, it is the work of dark magic, the work of the Dragon of Death acting somehow from the time in which she is imprisoned. I do not know how this is happening, but it must be stopped."

"I fear our clan is dead, or worse, having their life force sucked out of them to fuel this rampant dark magic," said Buttons.

For a moment, Billy again let himself imagine what it would be like to have his life force taken away and was filled with the same empty cold feeling.

Do not allow those thoughts, Spark told him. *They will weaken you, and you must be strong. Stronger than you've ever had to be. We need your strength, Billy.*

"With this much dark magic, the Noxious could bring the Dragon of Death back," said Xing. "We cannot let that happen."

Buttons turned to the children. "We thought we were asking you to join a war where we had an army, but it appears we are only four."

"Eight," said Charlotte in a loud, clear voice. "There are eight of us in this, not four."

"Charlotte's right," Billy said, buoyed by Charlotte's determination. "With us, you're stronger, aren't you? And we have powers, too. We're still with you."

He felt Spark's pride within him like a gentle glow.

"We need a new plan," thundered Tank. "We do not have the time or the luxury to mourn our lost friends. If anything, we owe it to them to do what they could not— to stop the dark magic that has poisoned our realm."

"We are greatly outnumbered," said Buttons. "And the nox-wings who did this are strong with dark magic."

"At least you, I mean we, have the element of surprise, don't we?" said Dylan.

"That is true," said Xing. "I propose we go straight to that wretched red dome and attack. They will not be expecting us. They won't know we are strengthened by human bonds and that our humans have powers."

"We can be your secret weapons!" said Ling-Fei.

"I had forgotten how hopeful humans could be," said Tank. "A stealth attack is a good start, but before we go to the red dome, we need more information."

"Silence," said Xing. "Someone is approaching."

A large, dark shape emerged from behind a boulder. It was a new dragon, almost as large as Tank. It had dark orange scales and a monstrous head with huge horns sprouting out of it.

Billy tensed and gripped tighter to Spark. But when he felt her relax, he relaxed with her. She must know this dragon.

"Dimitrius! Old friend, you are alive!" Buttons said, moving closer to the orange dragon. "I hope my human tongue approximation of your name suits? For our humans."

"I am indeed alive," said the orange dragon. "And, yes, that is fine. Always so considerate of the humans. I must say I'm surprised to see you four. And you have new names—Buttons, Spark, Xing, Tank."

Dylan leaned in near Buttons's ear and whispered loudly. "How does Dimitrius already know your names?"

"Names are a core part of a dragon's identity," replied

Buttons. "We can always tell the name of a dragon who has bonded with a human. Our bonded names give off a strength that other dragons can sense as clear as the colors of the sky."

"Why, that is a cute *human* you have there, Buttons," said Dimitrius, a wry grin touching his lips. "A bit weak, if I had to judge. But you've always had a soft spot for humans."

Billy felt Spark shift below him and sensed her growing wariness. Maybe this dragon wouldn't be so eager to help in the way they'd hoped. "We're sorry it took so long for us to get here," said Spark. "The Dragon of Death locked us in the mountain between the realms."

"Yes, I know about that," said Dimitrius.

"And you did not . . . try to rescue us?" said Buttons.

"I am sure he did," said Tank. "But remember, four human hearts were needed to open the mountain to the realms."

"Yes," said Dimitrius. "And you are back now."

Billy began to worry that maybe the dragons had been wrong to put so much faith in Dimitrius. He couldn't quite put his finger on it, but something was off about him—something he didn't like. He could sense Spark felt similarly.

"We are, but I fear it is too late," said Spark. "Dimitrius, what has happened? We saw the cave and the horror that was left behind. Did any of the clan survive the nox-wing attack?"

Dimitrius stared at Spark for a long moment. And then he let out a sound so horrifying that it took Billy a moment to realize it was a laugh. "A lot has changed since you left, *Spark*." Dimitrius spat on the ground as if saying the name left a bad taste in his mouth. "My priorities have . . . changed."

Electricity buzzed in the air around Spark. "What are you saying, Dimitrius? I saw a vision—the Dragon of Death is returning. The Noxious are growing in power. We must act quickly."

Dimitrius stepped closer. "You are right. The Great One, or 'the Dragon of Death,'t as you call her, is returning. I realized after you left how wrong we had been. The Great One had offered us power, and like fools we rejected it. I knew we had to bring her back. And that she would reward the nox-wings who could prove their loyalty." He turned a sharp eye on Spark and the other dragons. "I hope, of course, that you will join us."

"You've become a nox-wing!" Buttons exclaimed, horrified.

"We will *never* join the Dragon of Death," said Spark vehemently.

"I thought you might say that," said Dimitrius. He stood on his hind legs, extending his body to its full length. He looked skyward, holding out a paw and turning it to the sky. He seemed to be concentrating intensely, and his entire body quivered. Billy followed Dimitrius's gaze and gasped. One of the stars in the sky was hurtling toward them.

"Look out!" Billy shouted as the star shot into Dimitrius's open paw. Dimitrius lowered himself back to the ground, the star hovering above his right paw.

"Serving the Great One has its . . . benefits," he said with a devilish smile.

The air hummed with tension. Spark and the other dragons shifted into protective stances.

"Now, I am going to give you and your group one last chance. A *choice*. There will be a reckoning for those who have crossed the Great One. But for you, Spark, I think concessions can be made given our unique *history*. Your group, the humans included, can join the Noxious. We grow in strength every day, while the rest of the realm weakens and loses its power. Once the Great One has returned, we will fulfill her vision and rule both the Dragon Realm and the Human Realm. The choice is simple. Choose wisely. But know that you will help me whether you want to or not. I think you would rather be on my side."

This was not the battle that Billy had agreed to. Were they strong enough to face an entire army of evil dragons on their own? Could they win? Or had he joined the losing side in this war?

But he knew no matter what, he would never fight alongside the Dragon of Death. He'd seen Spark's vision on the ice wall. He would do everything he could to stop that from happening.

"How could you do this to us, Dimitrius? We were *friends*," said Buttons. "We discovered all of the realm together. I helped you collect your first hoard of limestones. We took our first flight together."

"Don't be foolish, *Buttons*," said Dimitrius with a sneer. He flicked his tongue out and narrowed his eyes.

"Although you always were the foolish one. Too soft. You would never have accomplished anything if it wasn't for me and those around you, helping you along."

"That is enough, Dimitrius," spat Spark, electricity still buzzing all around her. "We will *never* join the Dragon of Death and the Noxious. She is like a black hole, feasting on the power of others and the life force of all until there is nothing left. I am surprised you are so foolish to believe whatever she has promised. Your heart has been poisoned."

Dimitrius shifted his gaze to Spark. "It appears that you are the foolish one," he said. "You may have sent her back in time, but nothing can hold the Great One for long. She will return. And she *will* reward those loyal to her. Even from her distant time, she has already granted the nox-wings more power than you can comprehend. You think you are so strong with your human bonds, but you are no match for me."

In one fluid motion, Dimitrius tossed the star into the air, snatched it in his mouth with his powerful jaws, and swallowed. The glowing star sat in the center of his chest, and his body convulsed. Boils appeared all over his limbs, and his body distorted so that he barely looked like a dragon at all. Then Dimitrius began to grow. Everyone in the group retreated several steps as he grew taller and taller, his outstretched wings large enough to encompass the entire group. When he finally stopped growing, his body resumed its dragon shape, and his eyes glowed a dark purple. "You are all fools," he said. With a roar, he stomped on the ground, shaking everything in sight and sending peaches tumbling off the trees. In the distance, seven new dragons approached. Billy realized with growing horror that they must be other nox-wings.

Dimitrius opened his mouth and shot an avalanche of purple fire at the group.

The children screamed. Billy clutched Spark, hoping that their bond would bring him strength, but he only felt his own fear amplified.

Buttons shot out a protective dome above them, just in time to shield the group from the blast, though it wasn't enough to block all the flames. Great ropes of fire burst through the shield, hitting Xing. She gave an ear-piercing roar and reared sideways, almost sending Ling-Fei tumbling off.

"Xing!" Ling-Fei cried out.

"I'm okay," panted Xing. "Hold on!"

"This is terrible!" yelled Dylan, burying his face behind Buttons.

More fire burst through the protective dome with every passing second.

"Dylan!" Buttons shouted. "I need your help to keep the shield up! Focus on the bond."

Dylan nodded and looked toward the shield, his face contorting with effort. Billy saw that the shield was strengthening, and holes began to close. He had never seen so much chaos. It was evident that their dragons really did need them—Dylan's efforts were helping Buttons maintain the shield. Billy hoped he'd be able to help Spark when she needed him.

"You're doing it Dylan! Keep it up!" Billy shouted.

He looked back toward the horizon and saw that the nox-wings were almost upon them.

"What are we going to do?" cried Billy. "We're outnumbered!"

"Spark!" yelled Tank. "We're counting on you!"

Spark nodded and closed her eyes.

Billy, we don't have much time, said Spark inside his head. *I need you to help me stun the nox-wings so we can make an escape. Focus on our bond.*

This was it. This was his chance. Billy closed his eyes and concentrated. He felt the inner heat that Spark was channeling, and he tried with all his might to help her.

"Everyone, close your eyes!" shouted Spark. Her wings crackled, and she released a flash so bright and powerful that even behind closed eyes, Billy's vision went white. "Now!" shouted Spark. "Retreat!" He felt Spark lift into the air.

"Ling-Fei! Dylan! Charlotte! Are you all right?" Billy shouted, eyes still shut.

"I'm fine!" said Ling-Fei, "But I can't see."

"I can't see anything either!" said Dylan.

"Give it a second," said Charlotte. "My vision is just coming back."

"Well, what's happening?" yelled Dylan.

"We're getting away, but those nox-wings are close behind," said Charlotte.

"Not if we can help it!" shouted Xing, and with a burst of speed, the four kids and their dragons shot through the night sky.

CHAPTER 25
THE BATTLE

Wind chafed at Billy's knuckles and stung his eyes as they raced through the night. Far below, he could make out a sparkling lake filled with giant limestone pillars that poked through the water's surface like fingers. Balls of fire and ice shot past them, but Billy could sense the attacks before they reached him, and he helped Spark dodge any harm.

Looking over his shoulder, Billy saw Xing was falling behind.

"Faster, Xing!" cried Buttons. "The nox-wings are catching up!" Buttons flew with surprising speed and dexterity.

"I'm flying as fast as I can!" yelled Xing. A loud crack filled the air, followed by a roar from Xing and a scream from Ling-Fei.

Billy looked back. An ice boulder had struck them,

but the pair managed to stay together in the air. The group slowed down so they could catch up.

"Ling-Fei!" screamed Charlotte. "Are you all right?"

"I think my arm is broken," Ling-Fei said through gritted teeth.

"I, too, am injured," said Xing, clearly in pain. Gold blood dripped from a gash in her midsection. "We cannot outrun them for long."

"What are we going to do?" asked Charlotte.

"I've got an idea," said Xing, wincing as she spoke. "Follow me."

Xing and Ling-Fei turned downward and dove toward the lake. The others followed.

"Ling-Fei, I need your help!" yelled Xing, beams shooting from her eyes down to the lake. "Focus on our bond! I'm not strong enough on my own."

As they cut through the air, Billy saw the entire lake rise from the ground like an untethered balloon. It was as if the lake was falling upward—slowly at first, then faster with every inch it climbed.

"Hold your breath, children!" cried Xing as the water's surface approached. "And keep diving!"

Billy braced himself for impact as they shot into the lake like bullets. The water was cold, and he fought the urge to gasp. Then, without warning, they punched out of the water, suddenly suspended between the floating lake above and the empty lake bed below.

Billy stared, wide-eyed, at the suspended lake above them. Even after everything he'd seen since arriving at camp, he couldn't quite believe the sight of a *lake* floating in midair. Would it be enough? Or could Dimitrius and the nox-wings defeat anything with dark magic on their side? No, he couldn't think like that. He had to believe that he, his friends, and their dragons were strong enough to win. But even as he tried to rally his courage, he saw that Dimitrius and the nox-wings were already swimming through the floating lake above them, their expressions fierce through the distorted water.

"Quick, Spark, now is our chance," shouted Xing. Spark looked at Xing, confusion on her face. Dimitrius and the nox-wings were going to catch up any moment now, and even though their bonds made them stronger, Billy was worried about how well he would do in close combat. He knew he needed to use his wits to stay one step ahead of the enemy dragons. He looked up at the pursuing nox-wings cutting through the cold water and wondered how they could be stopped. He remembered Spark using her powers to trap them behind an ice wall when they first met. And then the thought came to him. *Spark, Xing wants us to freeze the nox-wings in ice!*

Brilliant, Billy! Suddenly, Billy felt an electric cool run through his veins. Bright blue beams of light shot out from Spark's eyes and into the lake above. He could feel Spark's ice powers. He focused on their task and helped Spark channel the blast at the nox-wings until they had captured them in a single sphere of ice, like a snow globe. The nox-wings crashed against the insides of the sphere, trying to break free.

"Well done," yelled Ling-Fei from astride Xing. As she spoke, the floating lake crashed down, plunging the children and their dragons momentarily in water before it returned to the dry earth beneath them. Dimitrius and the nox-wings remained frozen above them.

"Spark, Billy! Hold them for as long as you can," said Tank.

Spark nodded, beams still shooting from her eyes.

"We don't have much time," Billy said, his voice unsteady. He could feel how strong Dimitrius and the nox-wings were and that his and Spark's power was starting to falter in the face of it. It felt as though he'd been running for a very long time, and each step was harder than the last. "I don't think we can hold them off for much longer."

"I've never felt such strength," Spark ground out. "I thought only a human-dragon bond could bring that kind of power."

"Spark is right," said Tank. "The nox-wings are much stronger than we expected from the dark magic. We will need all our strength, and we must work together to defeat them."

"I can't fly much longer," said Xing. Her voice was weak. Suddenly her body slumped in the air, and she fell from the sky. Ling-Fei screamed, still on Xing's back. Billy cried out too, his heart plunging as his friend plummeted through the air. He wanted to go to them, but he knew he had to stay focused on holding the nox-wings in the ice.

Tank and Buttons lunged forward in a flash of red, green, and gold, catching Xing and Ling-Fei and flying them down to a limestone pillar.

Spark and Billy followed slowly. "Billy," said Spark quietly, "I know you're overwhelmed, but I need you. I can't do this on my own." The beams from her eyes flickered.

"Ling-Fei and Xing are both gravely injured," said Buttons. "It will take all my focus to heal them."

Tank nodded at Buttons. "Restore their strength, friend. As quickly as you can."

Buttons closed his eyes and went very still.

Billy felt the sound before he heard it. The pillar started to vibrate beneath them, rippling the water in the lake below and rattling his bones. A deep growl came from Buttons, almost like a purr, and it gave Billy renewed strength, which he channeled into his bond with Spark to keep the nox-wings imprisoned.

Buttons began to rock back and forth—first his head, then his arms, and then his entire body. The purr shifted into a flowing melody. He thumped his belly with his paws in time to the beat of the tune he was singing.

And then great clouds of golden smoke were flowing from Buttons's body toward Xing and Ling-Fei. As the golden smoke enveloped them, their wounds began to heal. With a crack, Ling-Fei's arm snapped from a crooked angle back to its original form. Xing's silver scales closed over the gaping gash in her side, as if it had never been there at all.

Billy was filled with an exhausted sense of relief. They could do this. They could *win*. When Buttons had restored Xing and Ling-Fei, their group would be at full strength. Together, they would defeat Dimitrius and the nox-wings.

Billy looked back toward the ice sphere and felt his stomach drop. Dimitrius was grinning and flapping his wings faster and faster. As he did, a huge ball of swirling purple fire formed in the water in front of him. His wings came together in a thunderous clap, hurling the fireball forward. The ball exploded against the inner wall of the ice sphere. Billy staggered as he felt the impact, trying with all his might to help Spark contain the nox-wings.

Until he couldn't anymore.

Because Dimitrius and the nox-wings had burst out of the ice and were coming straight at them.

CHAPTER 26
SEPARATED

"Everyone, fire!" roared Tank. "Use the bond!"

Billy felt a surge of determination in Spark as she lowered her head and aimed a river of electric ice at Dimitrius. Xing fired ice too, while Buttons and Tank blew massive columns of fire. Billy put all his effort into Spark's blast and hoped that it would be enough.

Dimitrius let out a laugh and began to furiously beat his wings again, creating another massive purple fireball. It streamed toward the kids and their dragons like a shooting star, consuming their blasts as if they were nothing.

Billy felt Spark's pure terror, and he grew cold all over. The fireball struck all four dragons, throwing the children off their backs. Billy crashed on top of the limestone pillar, the impact knocking the wind out of him. Charlotte rolled next to him, cradling her elbow.

Ling-Fei looked close to tears. Dylan's face was covered in scrapes, and his glasses were crooked.

All four dragons struggled to get back up from the blast.

Even with the bonds, Billy realized, they were not strong enough. Dimitrius knew it, too.

"You cannot win," boomed Dimitrius. "Following the Great One has given us powers this realm has never seen before." A sneer crossed his face. "But fortune is on your side. You are worth more to me alive than dead, and you will be spared for now." He bared his teeth in a wicked grin. "I thought we would need the life force of at least ten more dragons to bring back the Dragon of Death, but you four are more powerful than most dragons. How fitting that the four who sent the Dragon of Death away will be the ones used to bring her back."

He fired another ball of electricity that opened into an enormous net as it flew toward them.

"Children," Spark said with great effort, "get under my wing! Quickly!" Billy, Charlotte, Ling-Fei, and Dylan managed to shuffle under Spark's wing just before the electric net landed. Billy felt Spark's pain as it seared into her flesh and paralyzed her muscles. She let out an ear-piercing roar.

Billy, we cannot escape, Spark said. *The star has given Dimitrius too much power. You and the others can still get away.* She shot out a flat shard of ice that hovered next to Billy and the other children like a flying carpet. *Get on. The net is loose enough for you to slip out. Hurry, we don't have much time.*

We won't leave you! Billy replied.

You must. You are our only hope. Trust your instincts. You must find a way to stop Dimitrius from bringing back the Dragon of Death.

Billy knew Spark was right. He nodded at her, trying to hold back tears. *This isn't the end.*

He turned to his friends. "Everyone, get on the ice!"

"What? Why?" Charlotte asked.

"Just trust me," Billy said.

The kids jumped up, and as soon as they were on, Spark's eyes flashed a bright blue, and ropes of ice locked each of them to the floating plate.

Charlotte grasped at the ice around her waist. "What is this—?" Before she could finish, the ice lurched forward, slipped through the electric net, and shot off at great speed away from their dragons.

"Dimitrius!" shouted one of the nox-wings. "The children are getting away!"

"Don't fall for their distraction! The children won't get far on their own, if they even survive the night. And if they do, we'll kill them tomorrow. We can easily hunt them down."

That was the last thing Billy heard as he and his friends hurtled farther and farther and farther away from the dragons.

He felt the separation from Spark in his bones. He felt like he was being torn, like something had been ripped out from inside of him and was stretching farther than it ever should. It hurt his heart. But he trusted Spark, and Spark had sent them away for a good reason.

To protect them. And now everything was up to them—only they could save their dragons from Dimitrius and the Noxious.

"What did you do, Billy?" yelled Charlotte, the wind whipping her hair every direction. "We have to get back! We can't leave our dragons! We made a promise!"

"I'm sorry," said Billy, his heart heavy. "This is the only way we can escape and still help our dragons. At least now we have a chance of stopping the Dragon of Death."

"Billy's right," said Dylan. "Our dragons wouldn't have wanted us to be captured with them."

"But how are we going to find them?" asked Charlotte, glaring at Billy. "And who put you in charge? You can't make decisions for all of us!"

"Part of my bond with Spark is that when we're close, I can hear her thoughts," said Billy. "She told me to do this. We had to." But even as he said the words, he felt a sliver of doubt. Everything had happened so fast, and now he worried that maybe they should have stayed with their dragons. And he knew that Charlotte was hurting the way he was from being separated. But he still didn't like that she was angry at him.

"We will find them, Charlotte," said Ling-Fei. "We'll find them, and we'll save them. The bond will be our guide."

"Where is this thing even taking us?" said Charlotte, glaring at Billy. "Did Spark share that piece of information with you?"

"There wasn't time!" yelled Billy. "Would you rather

we'd been captured in that electric net? Got blasted, if we were lucky? But most likely have our life force sucked out and used for dark magic?"

Charlotte turned away with a huff.

Billy looked back at the dark, glimmering lake behind them, his teeth chattering from the cold, and hoped he'd made the right decision.

CHAPTER 27
WATCH OUT

The children could still hear a distant roar of dragons as the plate of ice landed on the far side of the lake shore and turned to water, setting them free.

"We have to find a way to get to them!" said Charlotte, running back to the edge of the lake. "What direction were they going in?"

"I don't know, but they are in pain," said Ling-Fei, wincing. "I can feel it."

"Me, too," said Billy. He reached out through the bond to Spark. He could feel the tether between them stretching more with every passing second. And while that meant that he felt less of her fear and pain, now he was feeling the emptiness that came from being separated.

"We have to go to the red dome! That must be where Dimitrius is taking them," said Charlotte.

"Oh, so we'll just waltz into the red dome, the hub

of dark magic, and say 'Hello, we'd like you to release our dragons, please,'" said Dylan. "We can't do that!"

"You'll never persuade them with that attitude, power or no power!" snapped Charlotte. "We can't give up on them!" Her face was bright red, and she looked like she was about to cry.

Ling-Fei went up and stroked her back. "We will come up with something, Charlotte. I know we will."

"Nobody is giving up on our dragons," said Billy, trying to stay calm. "But this is bigger than them. It's up to us to stop the Dragon of Death from returning."

Charlotte sniffed loudly. "You're right," she said. "This is all just . . . so much more intense than I thought it would be. I'm sorry for shouting at you, Dylan." She glanced over at Billy. "You. too. I know you were trying to help."

Billy nodded and patted her shoulder. "I get it," he said.

"Yeah, don't worry about it," said Dylan. "Anyway, I've got three sisters. I'm used to being shouted at. I want to be reunited with our dragons as much as you do."

"I know," said Charlotte. Then she looked up at Ling-Fei. "How is your arm, Ling-Fei?"

Ling-Fei swung her arm in a circle a few times. "It feels better," she replied. "Whatever Buttons did really helped." She moved next to Charlotte again. "I know how you feel. It's awful being separated."

Charlotte ran her hands through her hair a few times and took a couple of deep breaths. She turned toward them, putting her back to the lake. "We need to stay calm. The first thing we should do is to figure out which direction the red—"

"Charlotte," Billy said, looking over her shoulder, eyes narrowed, at the lake behind her.

"Billy, don't interrupt me," said Charlotte holding up her hand. "I'm making a plan—you aren't the only one who can come up with plans, you know—"

"Charlotte, watch out!" yelled Billy, lunging forward.

A giant sea crab the size of a small car emerged from the lake, grabbed Charlotte's ankle with its claw, and hoisted her upside down in the air.

"No!" yelled Billy, running after the crab as it turned to go back into the water. He reached it just before it submerged completely and grabbed hold of one of its back legs. Dylan and Ling-Fei were right behind him and grabbed on, too.

"PULL!" Billy yelled.

"I'm trying!" said Dylan.

"Hang on, Charlotte!" yelled Ling-Fei.

Billy pulled as hard as he could, but the crab was stronger. It went deeper and deeper into the lake, till the water rose above Billy's waist and the only sign of Charlotte was a wild thrashing below the surface and rapidly rising bubbles.

Billy felt as if he had a hole in his stomach. He tried to stay calm. He *had* to stay calm. If he panicked, they'd lose Charlotte for sure. But terror crept in with every second Charlotte was below the water. "Pull harder!" he shouted, but it was no use. They were losing more ground, and the water was almost at his shoulders. Ling-Fei took a deep breath as she went under, then burst back up.

"I had to let go! I'm sorry!" she cried.

Dylan went under next and came up sputtering, clutching his glasses to his face. He dove back down, trying to grab the crab's leg, but couldn't get a grip on it.

Billy fought hard. He held on and felt himself being pulled all the way under when suddenly, the thrashing stopped.

The crab kicked with a jolt of energy and sprung out of Billy's grasp.

"CHARLOTTE!" yelled Billy.

The crab was gone, and so was Charlotte.

CHAPTER 28
THE DEAD FOREST

The water went still, and Billy went numb.

He stumbled back until he could stand, trying to comprehend what had just happened.

"You should get out of there, Billy," said Dylan. "There's nothing we can do. She's gone."

His voice cracked.

Billy stared at the surface of lake, desperately scanning it for any sign of Charlotte. This couldn't be it. She couldn't be gone. Not Charlotte. He felt his heart in his throat. They'd come all this way. They were supposed to look out for each other. Although he had only known Charlotte for a few days, he felt so connected to her already. They should have been able to save her.

"Billy," Dylan said again, tugging on his arm. "We have to get out of here."

The water in front of them began to churn.

"BILLY, COME ON!" shouted Dylan. "Ling-Fei, quick, let's get back to shore!"

Suddenly a mass of wet blond hair popped up out of the water.

Charlotte.

"You're alive!" cried out Ling-Fei.

"We need to . . . get . . . out . . . of . . . here," panted Charlotte, coughing and gasping for air.

Billy and Dylan helped her back to shore, where Ling-Fei stood with her arms open. Charlotte stumbled toward her before collapsing onto the sand, clutching a bulbous black orb that looked like a bowling ball.

"Charlotte?" said Ling-Fei tentatively, pushing Charlotte's hair out of her face.

After a moment, Charlotte held up the black ball. "Always go for the eyes if you're in a pickle," Charlotte said with a wan smile. "Not allowed in jujitsu competitions, of course, but I know how to fight dirty when I need to." Then she turned on her side and threw up.

"Oh, no," said Dylan, going green. "Whenever I see someone being sick, I . . . ." He gagged and turned back to the lake.

After Charlotte and Dylan had finished throwing up, Charlotte flopped over on her back.

"Are you okay?" said Billy. He was overwhelmed with relief that Charlotte had survived, but he felt a stab of guilt that he hadn't been able to help keep her above water. He should have been able to. How were they going to defeat the Dragon of Death if they'd almost lost Charlotte to a giant crab?

"I'm definitely *not* okay," said Dylan, wiping his mouth. "What *was* that?"

"I think I'm fine." Charlotte said. She looked down. "That sucker really had a hold of my legs, though. Even with my strength, I couldn't get it off me. Thank goodness for these suits. I thought my legs would be broken for sure, but the suit didn't even tear."

"I'm sorry we let you go," Billy blurted. "We should have held on."

"Don't be ridiculous. I knew you held on as long as you could," said Charlotte.

"So you don't feel like we . . . abandoned you?" said Billy.

Charlotte shook her head emphatically. "Of course not! Now stop making this about you. I'm the one who almost got drowned by a crab."

Billy smiled. "I'm glad you're okay. Do you think you can walk?"

Charlotte sat up and slowly got to her feet. She shifted her weight between her legs, testing her strength. "I'm good, I think. But I could lie down for a bit. Can we find somewhere to rest?"

"That's the best idea I've heard in a while," said Dylan.

Billy looked around to get a better idea of where they were. While they'd been in immediate danger, he hadn't noticed their surroundings at all. Now he did.

Where the sandy banks of the enormous lake ended, a forest began.

A dead forest.

There were thousands of trees but not a single leaf or living thing on any of them. Not even any peaches. Up above them, the three full moons still sat in the purple sky.

"We should get away from the lake," said Billy. "Who knows what else might be in there? And I don't think we should stay out in the open tonight. You heard Dimitrius—he's sending nox-wings to hunt us down."

"He was fairly confident we wouldn't survive the night. I'm guessing he knew about those crab things," said Dylan. "Horrible evil dragon."

"If we're going to find shelter, we should at least start going in the direction of the red dome," said Billy. "Ling-Fei, can you sense its direction from here?"

Ling-Fei paused, sort of sniffing the air. "It's south," she said. "Through these trees." She wrinkled her nose. "It smells like death. I'm not sure if it is the forest or the red dome itself." She tilted her head to the side. "And if we're going to find shelter, we should hurry."

"Why? Are those horrible nox-wings back?" asked Dylan, looking up at the sky.

"No, I don't think so," said Ling-Fei. "But it is going to rain." As she spoke, a huge raindrop, large enough to drench a whole person, fell from the sky. They all leaped back as the drop hit the earth, splashing everywhere.

"Into the forest we go, then," said Billy. "There has to be somewhere we can rest."

"And get out of this rain," added Charlotte. "With our luck it's probably acid rain or something awful."

"Everything in that forest is dead!" sputtered Dylan.

"There aren't even any immortal peach trees! And you heard Ling-Fei—it smells like death. How do we know we won't die as soon as we enter?"

"I'd rather take my chances with some dead trees than giant crabs," said Charlotte. "I never want to see a crab again unless it is on my plate and smothered in butter," she added with a shudder.

"The forest feels . . . empty," said Ling-Fei. "Dead, but empty. I think Billy is right. This is the way to go."

"Let's stay together and stay alert," said Billy. "Hopefully the trees will also give us a little bit of cover from any nox-wings flying overhead."

Despite Ling-Fei's reassurances, Billy couldn't help looking over his shoulder with almost every step he took. It was creepy being among the spindly dead trees. Branches clawed at his hair, and dead twigs snapped underfoot. The moonlight cast strange purple-tinted shadows. Billy hoped he'd made the right decision by leading them into the forest.

They walked in silence, saving their energy and staying focused in case of any surprises. The giant raindrops began to fall with more regularity, one almost soaking Dylan. Finally, after what felt like hours, they emerged from the forest.

And stood at the edge of a mountain range.

"There is no way we're going into those mountains tonight," said Dylan.

"Look!" said Ling-Fei, pointing. Just ahead of them, at the base of the nearest mountain, was a small cave.

"How do we know that isn't something else's shelter?" said Dylan.

"I can't sense anything," said Ling-Fei. "Come on, follow me."

"You better be right," said Charlotte.

The cave was empty.

"I told you," said Ling-Fei with a smile. "I think it's cozy!"

"*Cozy* is one word for it," said Charlotte, glancing around the barren cave.

The four collapsed on the cave floor. Now that they had a safe place to hide, Billy realized how tired he was, how much his whole body ached. He leaned back, putting his hands out behind him to support his weight.

"Tomorrow, we keep going toward the red dome," he said.

"That's if we make it until tomorrow," said Dylan, throwing his hands up into the air. "I mean, *anything* could pop in here and eat us."

"Dylan," said Ling-Fei in a soothing voice. She moved to face Dylan and took his hands in hers. "Everything is going to be okay. Here, look me in the eyes." Ling-Fei paused and waited for Dylan to follow her instructions. "Take a deep breath and repeat after me." Dylan breathed in deeply with Ling-Fei. Then she said very slowly, "Everything. Is. Going. To. Be. Okay."

"Everything. Is. Going. To. Be. Okay," repeated Dylan, emphasizing each word like Ling-Fei. "Everything is going to be okay," he said again. He took another deep breath. "You're right. We're all in one piece; we have each other; we're out of the open . . . I guess we're as safe as we're going to be." Dylan sat down and slipped his backpack off his shoulders before pulling out a couple of peaches. "And we've got some food."

Billy smiled at Dylan. "You sure love peaches." He shuffled closer to Dylan and took a peach from his hand.

"Who wouldn't?" said Dylan. "If we eat enough of these we might find one that makes you *immortal*. Maybe then I'd be more keen to take on that dragon that *swallows stars* or even the Dragon of Death." He took a bite, spraying peach juice everywhere. "Plus, they are the best peaches I've ever had."

"I can't believe you and Xing lifted an entire lake out of the ground," said Charlotte, biting into a peach. "And I thought *I* was strong."

"Hopefully our dragons are safe," said Billy. A thread of unease unspooled itself through him. He hated thinking about Spark having her life force drained or being in any kind of pain. He didn't know how long it would take to fully take a dragon's life force. He just hoped they would arrive in time.

They were silent for a long moment.

"What are we going to do?" Dylan asked.

"Same thing we were always going to do here in the Dragon Realm," said Billy. "Stop the Dragon of Death. And save our dragons along the way."

"Ah, well, yes, that is an excellent big picture plan, but I'm a bit of a details guy."

"I have no idea!" Billy burst out. "How can I know what we are supposed to do when we don't know anything?"

"Exactly!" said Dylan. "That's what I'm trying to say."

"What are our other options?" said Charlotte. "It isn't like we can just go home."

"Do you guys wish we could?" said Dylan, looking at them with wide eyes. "Go home? Pretend this all never happened?"

"I'm scared," admitted Billy. "But I don't want to abandon our dragons. And I don't want to give up. Dylan, we have a chance to save . . . everything. We've got to keep going."

"I'd feel better about that if we knew what we were going to do."

"I agree with Dylan," said Ling-Fei softly. "We need some sort of plan."

"Okay, what about this?" said Billy, thinking quickly. "We get to the red dome, scope it out, figure out what we're dealing with, and then make a plan of action. At the very least we can find our dragons. Once we're reunited, we'll be more prepared. And they'll know more than us."

"If they haven't had all their life force sucked out of them," said Charlotte darkly.

"We'd know if that happened," said Billy. "We'd feel it." At least he hoped they would. He could just barely feel the bond between him and Spark, but he told himself that as long as he could feel something, that meant she was still alive. When they'd first been separated from the dragons, the pain had been piercing. But slowly it had numbed to more of a dull, persistent ache. It almost felt like his heart had gone to sleep the way his arm would when he slept on it.

"As far as plans go, that one is pretty shaky," said

Dylan. "But it is better than nothing." He yawned. "And maybe one of us will have a genius idea after we get some sleep."

Billy smiled, glad to have Dylan feeling hopeful again. "That is the kind of attitude we need. I'm sure one of us will come up with *something*." Then he looked at the others. You all get some rest. I'll stay up and keep watch."

"That's a good idea to have a lookout," said Charlotte. "We should take turns. Are you sure you want to do the first watch?"

"Yeah, of course," said Billy. Even though he was exhausted, he didn't think he'd be able to sleep. Despite what he'd told his friends, he was terrified of all the unknowns, about what might happen when they reached the red dome. If they ever reached it. He might as well make himself useful and keep watch.

"All right," said Charlotte. "Wake me up when you want to sleep. I'll take the second watch."

She went farther into the cave with Dylan and Ling-Fei, and the three of them lay down on the cave floor.

There was a long silence.

"Good night, y'all," said Charlotte.

"Good night," said Dylan.

"Good night," said Billy.

"Wan-an," said Ling-Fei, using the Chinese phrase for *good night*. She patted the floor of the cave. "Good night to you, too. Please protect us up here. You seem like a good cave. I think we'll be safe here."

"I don't think the cave can understand you," said Dylan with a yawn.

"I just want it to know we appreciate it," said Ling-Fei sleepily.

Billy sat by the cave opening, gazing up at the three full moons. He let out a long, deep breath and rolled his shoulders back. Now that it was just him, and him alone, he didn't have to act brave. "I hope you're okay, Spark," he whispered.

There was no reply.

CHAPTER 29
DOWN THE RIVER

"Wake up!"

Billy's eyes flew open, and he sat up straight, adrenaline pumping through his veins. Was something wrong?

Ling-Fei was standing next to him looking outside the cave. She turned to smile at him. "It's sunrise! Time to go! We need to make the most of the daylight," she went on. "The days are shorter here. I'll wake the others."

"Good idea," said Billy, stretching his arms over his head. "The sooner we get going, the better." His body ached. He felt like he could sleep for at least another twelve hours. He'd been anxious the entire time he'd kept watch, jumping at every shadow. When he'd been unable to keep his eyes open and kept dozing off, he'd woken Charlotte to take over the watch. But despite being exhausted, he hadn't slept well at all. He'd had terrible nightmares. He couldn't remember exactly what he'd dreamed about, but the feeling of terror remained.

"I'm up, I'm up," said Dylan as Ling-Fei shook his shoulders. "We can't stay in here, our nice safe cave, a little longer?" he said, yawning.

"You'd rather we were out at night? In the dark?" asked Charlotte, brows raised. She'd popped up as soon as Ling-Fei had nudged her.

"All right, all right. Off into the unknown, probably to our deaths, we go," said Dylan.

After a breakfast of peaches and pork buns, the four climbed out of the cave. As they did, Ling-Fei patted it again. "Thank you for protecting us," she said. She looked at everyone else expectantly. "Say thank you," she said.

Feeling silly but not wanting to upset Ling-Fei, Billy gave the cave a thumbs-up. "Thanks," he said. Charlotte and Dylan did the same.

They stood at the edge of the mountain range, heads tipped back to gauge how high the peaks reached. In the daylight, they could better see how forbidding the range appeared. The mountains were inky black, like smoke smudges against the red sky.

"So do we go up and over?" Dylan asked after a moment. "Too bad none of us got flight as our power."

"To be fair, we thought we'd be able to fly on our dragons," said Charlotte.

"There has to be a way to go through them," Billy said, eyeing the mountains ahead. He, too, felt daunted by how far they would have to travel on foot. He had a terrible feeling it was going to take them days to reach the red dome. By then, it might be too late. If they made it at all.

Suddenly Ling-Fei got down on her hands and knees and put her ear on the ground.

"*Erm.* What are you doing down there?" asked Dylan, looking alarmed.

"*Shh!*" said Ling-Fei, "I'm listening."

"To what?" Dylan said.

Charlotte thwacked Dylan on the arm. "Shush! Let her listen."

After a minute Ling-Fei looked up and smiled. "There's a river that cuts through the mountains. It flows south, toward the red dome. If we follow it, I bet we'll get through to the other side."

"And you know this how?" Dylan said incredulously.

"Because of her *power*, you pickle-brain," snapped Charlotte.

"I heard the river in the earth," said Ling-Fei patiently. "I think this is the right way to go."

Billy was glad that somebody had an idea of what to do. "Then that's what we'll do," he said definitively. "We have to trust each other. And our powers. It's the only way we're ever going to get to the red dome."

Ling-Fei was right.

The group only had to walk about half a mile before they came upon a river that made a natural pass through the mountain range. Its banks were steep and narrow, but it was still better than attempting to climb the towering mountains around them. They hiked in silence along the riverbank for most of the day, walking in single file with Ling-Fei at the front and Charlotte at the back. As they marched on, Billy started to feel like they would never get out of the inky mountain range. That he'd spend the rest of his life walking along this river, surviving on nothing but peaches—the peach trees that had disappeared in the dead forest had reemerged alongside the river. Billy's earlier confidence in Ling-Fei and her power began to waver. Sure, she'd been right about there being a river, but did she know how far it went? And in what direction? He wanted to believe her one hundred percent, but as the day went on, doubts kept wiggling into his brain. It didn't help that Ling-Fei kept stopping to examine rocks, speaking to some and collecting others in her pockets as they went.

Twice, they saw nox-wings flying overhead and had to duck behind boulders, waiting, breathless, hoping they hadn't been discovered.

Billy had lost track of how long they'd been walking when they finally stopped underneath a peach tree to rest and have lunch, all sunburned and hungry.

"I'm exhausted," said Dylan, opening his backpack and passing around some pork buns.

"I don't think I'll ever get tired of pork buns," said Charlotte as she took a big bite.

"That's good," said Dylan, "because that and peaches are all we have."

Billy stretched his legs out in front of him as he sat and ate a peach. He didn't think his body had ever felt so sore. "Hopefully we'll get out of these mountains tonight," he said. "And closer to the red dome."

"Hopefully," Charlotte echoed.

"Hey, what's that?" asked Dylan, pointing to a gray blob in the river.

The group stood up and took several steps back.

"It might be another crab," said Charlotte, picking up a nearby stick.

But the animal that hopped out of the water looked nothing like a crab. Billy thought it was more of a mix between a small dog and a fish. Its face was scrunched between two big eyes, and it had a squat body with four stubby legs underneath and a small tail that waggled furiously as it hopped up and down on the shore. A big tongue hung out of its open mouth.

"It's a little river pup!" said Ling-Fei, walking toward it.

"You know what that animal is?" asked Billy. "I've never seen anything like it!"

Ling-Fei laughed. "Neither have I, but can't you tell it's a river pup? What else would it be? You're a good river pup, aren't you?" she cooed, going closer.

"Careful, Ling-Fei," said Dylan, taking a few steps back.

"I can tell this creature is gentle," said Ling-Fei. She walked right up to the animal and picked it up. "Hi, little one!"

The animal gave a small yap and licked Ling-Fei's face before squirming out of her grasp. It hopped up and down a few more times, then trotted toward Dylan.

Dylan let out a yell and ran around the group in a circle as the animal chased him.

"Relax, Dylan!" said Ling-Fei with a smile. "I bet it just wants one of the pork buns."

Dylan grabbed a pork bun and turned to look at the creature. He moved the bun in a large circle in front of him. The river pup followed the bun's movements with its whole head.

"Aha!" said Dylan. "It's the pork bun you're after, isn't it? Not me."

Dylan slowly crept forward with the pork bun extended in front of him.

When Dylan was a few paces away, the river pup leapt up and snatched the bun out of his hand, swallowing it whole. It gave a satisfied yap and hopped directly at Dylan, who caught the pup in his arms instinctively.

"Now you want to cuddle it?" asked Billy.

"I couldn't help it! It was looking at me with those big eyes. Ling-Fei is right," said Dylan, as the animal nuzzled his chest. "This little pup is sweet."

"I knew it," said Ling-Fei.

Charlotte looked on warily. "I don't know," she said. "My mama always said not to pick up strays you find in the street because you don't know where they've been."

The animal yapped again and licked Dylan on the cheek, leaving a trail of saliva. Dylan made a disgusted face, and the other three laughed out loud. It felt good to laugh. It melted some of the tension of feeling lost without their dragons and reminded Billy that even though they didn't have much of a plan, at least he wasn't alone.

The river pup continued to nuzzle Dylan, nosing around on his chest. Dylan laughed harder. "That tickles!"

Still laughing, Billy watched the strange creature press its nose harder against Dylan's chest. The Granite Pearl began to emerge out of the top of Dylan's suit, and as it did Billy realized with a sharp pang what was about to happen. It was like the moment before a falling glass shatters.

"Dylan! Your pearl!" he said, lunging toward Dylan. But it was too late. The animal grabbed the Granite Pearl in its mouth and leaped out of Dylan's arms. The chain around Dylan's neck snapped, and the pearl went with the river pup.

Billy felt like everything was moving in slow motion, like he was trapped in a bad dream. He knew how much they needed the pearls—not only to help them stay alive in this dangerous world but also to have a chance at defeating the Dragon of Death.

"No!" yelled Dylan.

"Get it!" said Charlotte.

They chased the river pup as it ran back to the river. It glanced over its shoulder at them and then jumped in, swimming downstream with its head above water.

"We're never going to be able to keep up!" said Dylan, running along the edge of the river.

"Billy, you're a surfer, right?" Charlotte asked between panting breaths.

"Yeah," said Billy, keeping his eyes on the river pup.

"So you're a good swimmer?" said Charlotte.

"Sure," said Billy, "But there's no way I can swim fast enough to catch that thing."

"Do you trust me?" she asked.

"Of course," Billy said.

Without warning, Charlotte picked Billy up by his waist and spun around twice.

"What are you doing, Charlotte?" Billy yelled.

"Try to keep your body straight and stiff," she said. And she flung Billy into the sky.

Billy cut through the air like a javelin. "Great thinking!" Billy yelled as he used his new agility skills to fly through the air and keep himself on track.

"You can do it, Billy!" yelled Charlotte. "Go! We'll catch up with you!"

Billy sliced into the water just behind the river pup. He swam as fast as he could, but as hard as he tried, he couldn't reach it. His arms and legs grew heavy, and he knew he'd have to stop and rest soon. Then, as the river pup was almost out of sight, it leaped out of the water and dashed into a cave at the side of the river.

"I'm going to follow it!" Billy shouted over his shoulder, hoping his friends could still hear him as they fell farther and farther behind. Billy swam until he reached the cave entrance, pulled himself up on the riverbank, and warily went in.

The cave was huge and completely empty apart from a large pile of rocks in the middle. The river pup was running around the rocks, yelping and looking remarkably pleased with itself.

"You are a naughty river pup," said Billy, walking up to it. Then something caught his eye. "What's this?" Behind the rocks was a jumble of random items, including a large claw, a bloody fang, a gold coin the size of Billy's palm, and, most importantly, the Granite Pearl. The river pup barked twice, and Billy could have sworn it grinned. "Sorry, buddy, you can't keep this," he said, reaching for the pearl.

As his hands closed around it, there was a loud scraping sound. Billy looked over his shoulder and let out a yell.

CHAPTER 30
A BARGAIN

Walking toward him was the strangest creature Billy had ever seen. It was made entirely of rocks, with distinctive legs and arms that were covered in moss and barnacles. An almost-human face stared out from its large rock head. As it scraped its way toward Billy, he could tell it was angry.

"MINE!" it roared, charging straight at him.

Billy dropped the Granite Pearl immediately and jumped to the side.

The rock creature practically dove into its pile of treasure. It stared at Billy, who now found himself trapped between it and the back of the damp cave.

The river pup ran up to the rock creature and started wagging its tail, clearly proud of having found and fetched the Granite Pearl.

"Billy! Did you find the pearl? I can't believe that little rascal stole it!" Dylan said as he and the others reached the cave entrance.

"Don't come in here!" Billy shouted. "It's not safe!"

"What do you mean, not safe?" Charlotte shouted back. "Are you okay?"

"I'm not sure!" Billy yelled.

The rock creature was still staring at him. The more Billy looked at it, the more he thought it looked like a troll, or what he imagined a troll would look like, at least. A rock troll.

"Well, this is ridiculous," he heard Charlotte mutter. "Either you are okay or you aren't." Her voice rose. "We're coming in! I've got a stick!"

As Billy's friends charged in, the rock troll stood up and roared. Charlotte, Ling-Fei, and Dylan slid to a stop, mouths open.

"What is *that*?" said Dylan.

"I think it is some kind of troll," Billy called from behind it.

"Is it . . . friendly?" asked Dylan, taking a few steps back.

"I don't know. It definitely doesn't want me taking any of its stuff. And it seems to think it owns the pearl now."

Billy wasn't sure what the rock troll wanted, but he sensed that it wasn't going to let him go without a fight. It seemed that it liked to collect things, and Billy worried that he was now part of its collection. At least it hadn't tried to kill him. Yet.

Very slowly, Ling-Fei took a smooth stone from her pocket and held it out to the rock troll. "For you," she said.

The rock troll snatched it with its gnarled rocky fingers and tossed it onto its pile.

"Is that . . . its hoard?" said Charlotte. "Like the dragons have?"

"I think so," said Billy.

"NOT like dragon hoard," the rock troll roared.

"You can talk?" said Dylan. He cleared his throat. "Hello, I'm Dylan O'Donnell," he said slowly. "We come in peace."

"It's not an alien," said Charlotte.

"No, it's just a pile of walking, talking rocks. Much more normal than an alien," said Dylan. "Guys, we've got to get my pearl back. Otherwise I'll be extra useless."

"I was trying to get it back," said Billy through clenched teeth. "But right now I think we need to focus on getting *me* back, and then the pearl." Then he looked up at Dylan. "And you aren't useless."

"I've got an idea," said Ling-Fei suddenly. She went closer and nodded her head toward the rock troll's hoard. "Your hoard is very nice," she said.

The rock troll nodded. "MINE."

"Right, I know," said Ling-Fei. She glanced at Billy, who was still trapped in the corner. "Can you get out from behind it?"

"I don't want to risk making it mad," said Billy.

"It doesn't think that . . . *you* are part of its hoard now, does it?" asked Charlotte, looking the most panicked since they walked in.

"I really hope not," said Billy. He cleared his throat. "Um, excuse me," he said, taking a small step forward.

The rock troll whirled around surprisingly fast for something so large and cumbersome. "BACK!" it roared.

Billy stepped back. He was suddenly worried that the rock troll might want him in its collection alive *or* dead. He very much wanted to stay alive.

Charlotte swore.

Dylan put his head in his hands.

Ling-Fei took a step closer.

"You can understand us, can't you?" she said softly.

The rock troll nodded.

"Let me try," said Dylan, stepping forward. "Hello . . . Mr. Rock Man."

"Not a man," growled the rock troll.

"Erm, Rock Woman," Dylan tried again.

"Not woman," said rock troll.

"Right. Hello . . . Rock," said Dylan. "Do you fancy letting my friend Billy go?"

The rock troll growled.

"I don't think this is going to work," said Dylan, taking a step back.

"You don't have your pearl, pickle-brain," muttered Charlotte. "That is the whole reason we are here."

"Oh, yeah!" said Dylan, patting his chest where the pearl usually sat. "Still worth a shot, though." He looked at Charlotte. "Why don't you rip it apart? You've still got *your* pearl."

"I'm not THAT strong," said Charlotte. "Do you see this thing?"

"Guys, can you figure out whatever it is you are going to do?" said Billy from behind the rock troll.

Ling-Fei stepped forward. "That is our friend," she said, pointing at Billy. "You can't keep him." Then she pointed at the Granite Pearl. "And you can't keep that either."

The rock troll growled again.

Ling-Fei held up her hands in a pacifying gesture. "Don't worry, we won't just take either from you. Maybe we can do a trade?"

The rock troll's beady black eyes lit up. "Trade?" it asked. "What do you have?"

"Dylan," hissed Charlotte. "Get the pork buns."

"We only have three left!"

"*Dylan*. It's your pearl!"

"And my life," added Billy. "Worth more than three pork buns, I hope."

Dylan unzipped his backpack and took out a pork bun. He handed it to Ling-Fei, who held it out.

The rock troll shook its head and spat in disgust.

The pork bun went back in the backpack.

"What else do we have?" Charlotte asked, her voice high.

Ling-Fei reached into her pocket and took out a few more rocks that she'd collected along the river. "Do you like these?" she said.

The rock troll nodded. "But can get anywhere."

"I see," she said. "You want something . . . rare."

"Yes. Like this." The rock troll held up the Granite Pearl.

"We're never getting my pearl back, are we?" moaned Dylan.

"Right now I'm more worried about getting *Billy* back," said Charlotte.

"Too bad we can't just give the rock troll a piece of Billy, you know as a souvenir or something," said Dylan.

"That's genius!" Billy burst out.

"You aren't going to cut off your finger or anything like that, are you?" said Dylan.

"Not exactly, but maybe I can give it a tooth."

At the word tooth the rock troll swiveled its head around. "TOOTH?" it boomed. Billy noticed in that moment that the rock troll itself had no teeth inside its wide gaping rock mouth.

"Yes," said Billy. "You can have my tooth. If you let me go. Trade."

The rock troll seemed to consider it. "Good trade," it said. "I take tooth." It came closer to Billy.

"Is it just going to rip a tooth straight out of Billy's head?" whispered Dylan, sounding horrified. Despite being the one to suggest it, Billy also started to feel a bit horrified by what was about to happen.

"Shut up, Dylan," said Charlotte. "You can do this, Billy. I once had a tooth knocked out in a jujitsu competition; you'll be fine."

"Open mouth," said the rock troll.

"This one," said Billy, pointing at one of his bottom front teeth. He didn't want it to take a molar or one from the top. Then he closed his eyes.

His mouth was suddenly full of rocky gnarled fingers. He felt them grind against his teeth and then pause over one of his bottom teeth.

"Mine," said the rock troll, and tugged.

"OW!" Blood filled Billy's mouth.

The tooth came out faster than he'd thought it would. But as his tongue probed the spot where his tooth had just been, he realized that there were *two* teeth missing.

"You took two!" Billy said, spitting blood.

The rock troll shrugged. "Accident," he said. "My fingers big. Your teeth small."

"Give me the pearl, then," said Billy. "You took two teeth. I should get two things. Two for two, right?"

The rock troll seemed to consider this. "Okay," it said. "Fair." It tossed Billy the pearl and put Billy's two teeth in his own mouth. "Mine."

"Yep, they are your teeth now," said Billy, stepping out from around the hoard and next to his friends. He handed Dylan the pearl. Dylan breathed a sigh of relief. "I missed this," he said. He looked up at the rock troll. "Pleasure doing business with you," he said.

"Easy for you to say," muttered Billy, wincing as he wiped blood from his mouth. "You didn't have to give up any teeth."

"You have to admit, it did some pretty good negotiating. Surprisingly smart for a pile of sentient rocks," said Dylan.

"I VERY SMART," roared the rock troll.

The children backed up. "That's what I said, pal," said Dylan. "Smart."

"Can we get out of here before it decides it wants something else from us?" asked Charlotte. "I've got an award-winning smile. I don't want that thing to take any of *my* teeth."

"Don't have to tell me twice," said Dylan, quickly walking back out into the light.

"You are very smart," Ling-Fei said to the rock troll as she followed Charlotte and Dylan out of the cave.

With one last look at his teeth in the rock troll's mouth, Billy ran after his friends.

CHAPTER 31
A RIDE IN THE SKY

Billy's mouth ached and tasted like blood. As they walked back along the riverbank, he kept spitting, trying to clear the copper taste.

He still felt jittery from the encounter with the rock troll. In the moment, offering his tooth had seemed like a brilliant idea, but now that they were out of immediate danger and had Dylan's pearl back, he realized just how much might have gone wrong. What if the thing had ripped off his entire head? Billy shuddered.

"Good job in there, Billy," said Dylan, like he knew what Billy was thinking. "You really saved the day."

"Excuse me," said Charlotte. "I think you'll find it was a team effort." But she was smiling as she said it, and with the support of his friends, Billy started to feel calmer.

They continued to walk along the river all afternoon and into the early evening, still keeping a careful watch out for enemy dragons and any other danger.

As the sun started to sink behind the black mountains, Dylan sighed. "Can we take a break? I'm tired."

"We need to find somewhere to hide for the night before it gets too dark," said Billy. "But I get it. I'm tired, too."

"We're all exhausted," said Charlotte.

"I don't think I've ever walked so much," said Ling-Fei. "And I love going walking in the forest."

"It isn't just . . . being tired," Dylan said slowly. "I miss home. Not camp. Home home. Ireland home." He paused. "We will go home, won't we?" he added. "After all this?"

"Of course we'll go home," said Charlotte. "Stop being such a pessimistic possum."

"I'm not even sure I know what a possum is," said Dylan. "But seriously, do you guys think we're going to make it out of here alive?"

Billy looked up into the twilight. "I hope so," he said.

They all were silent for a long moment.

"We still want to do this, don't we?" said Ling-Fei quietly. "Our dragons would understand if we turned back."

"If we turn back, we'll lose everything anyway," said Billy. "We're what our dragons need to defeat the Dragon of Death. The world we know, everyone we know— *everything*—will be destroyed if we don't stay and help."

"If I have a choice, I'd probably choose to have the world end while I'm in my own bed, fast asleep. Instead of, you know, being eaten alive by a dragon," said Dylan wryly.

"We can go back, if you really want," said Billy slowly. "I don't want to force anyone to do anything they don't want to do."

"And know that I was dooming the entire world, both human and dragon?" Dylan cracked a smile. "Can't have that, can we?"

Billy grinned at his friend and slung his arm around Dylan's shoulder. "That's the spirit," he said. Being brave for Dylan and his friends was easier than being brave by himself. Despite his confident words, a small part of Billy wondered if they even had a chance of saving their dragons. Saving the world. Maybe they weren't the right ones for this. Maybe the mountain shouldn't have opened for them. Billy pushed the thought out of his head. He had to try. He was here now. He couldn't let his fear get the best of him.

"If we're done with our little pep talk, can we keep walking, please? It's getting darker by the minute," said Charlotte, looking over her shoulder. "I don't want to know what comes out at night around here."

"Ling-Fei," said Billy, an idea occurring to him. "You know how you . . . sensed where the river was? And sensed that the cave was empty last night?"

She nodded.

"Do you think you could find us an empty cave to sleep in?"

Ling-Fei's eyes lit up. "I can try," she said. And then she promptly lay down on the earth and closed her eyes.

The other three waited in silence. If this didn't work, Billy wasn't sure what they were going to do tonight.

Then Ling-Fei sat up and pointed up. "There! See that small opening? I don't sense anything in it."

"So . . . how do we get up there?" said Dylan, squinting at where Ling-Fei had pointed.

"Climb," said Billy.

"Easy for you to say, backflip boy," said Dylan. "Unless I can charm the mountain to bend down for me, I don't know how I'm going to get up."

"Let me go first," said Billy. "I'll scout it out and try to find the easiest way."

He quickly realized there *was* no easy way. Even with his new agility skills, he struggled to find footholds and nearly slipped several times.

There was no way the others would be able to climb it.

When he finally got there, he was relieved to see that the cave was empty and just big enough for the four of them. It was barely a cave, more of a hidey-hole tucked away in the mountainside. It would be the perfect place to sleep—if only the others could reach it.

Then he had an idea.

"Hey, Charlotte," Billy called down. Charlotte stared up at him in the darkening light. "How far do you think you can toss Dylan?"

Charlotte grinned up at Billy. "Farther than I can throw you."

"I do not like where this is going," said Dylan.

"It's the only way up," said Billy.

Dylan sighed. "Fine. But you'd better catch me!"

"I promise," said Billy.

"If I'm going to be a human elevator service, you could be a little more grateful about it," grumbled Charlotte as she squatted down and put her hands out for Dylan to step onto.

"You have literal super-strength," said Dylan. "It's the least you can do."

"Up you go!" said Charlotte, and threw Dylan into the air. Billy reached out, grabbing Dylan and pulling him into the small cave.

"Got him!" Billy said. "Send Ling-Fei on up!"

Charlotte tossed Ling-Fei the same way she had done with Dylan. "Now how do I get up?" she mused.

"Try jumping," said Billy. "I bet you can jump pretty high with super-strength."

Charlotte grinned. "Billy Chan, you are smarter than I give you credit for." She crouched down low and burst up into the air like there was a rocket beneath her.

"Quick, grab her!" said Ling-Fei. Billy and Dylan grabbed Charlotte as she flew toward them and pulled her into the cave, knocking into Ling-Fei. They all tumbled to the ground in a heap.

Billy began to laugh first. And then they were all laughing. Laughing till their stomachs hurt and they had tears running down their faces.

"What a day," said Billy when he could finally speak.

"Understatement of the century," said Dylan.

"I don't think I've ever been so tired," said Charlotte with a yawn.

"Do you think the dragons are okay?" said Ling-Fei.

"I think so," said Billy. "I think we'd feel it if something were really wrong. Like . . ." He let his voice trail off. At least this was what he kept telling himself. He had to believe in the bond.

"Like what?" prompted Dylan.

"Like if they were killed," said Charlotte matter-of-factly.

"Charlotte!" said Ling-Fei.

"What? That's what we're all worried about. We might as well say it. No sense in giving a fear more power over us by not naming it. That's what my grandma always says."

"As long as the dragons stay alive, and we stay alive, we're fine," said Billy.

"Easy-peasy," said Dylan.

"I just hope they can stay alive until we reach them," said Ling-Fei, looking worried. "The red dome is still so far."

If Ling-Fei said the red dome was far, it must be. Billy felt overwhelmed by the weight of what they needed to do. Would they *ever* reach the red dome? No, he couldn't think like that. He refused to. He looked at his friends.

"Well, then we need to rest tonight so we can get an early start tomorrow," he said with as much authority as he could muster. "We'll go as far as we can. And then we'll do the same the next day, and the next, till we get there. That's the best we can do."

"What if our best isn't good enough?" said Dylan.

"It's all we've got," said Billy. "Now come on, let's get some sleep."

Billy woke with a start.

The cave was *shaking*.

Dylan was lying on the ground next to him, snoring, and Charlotte was sprawled out in the middle of the cave. Ling-Fei crouched near the entrance, her hand on the cave wall to steady herself.

"What's going on?" Billy cried, leaping up. He heard a faint but deep cracking that sounded like boulders ripping apart. As he reached the edge of the cave, his stomach rose up into his throat like he was on a roller coaster. They were somehow being lifted hundreds of feet up into the air.

Ling-Fei turned to him with huge eyes. "I . . . I asked the cave for help," she said. "And I think it listened."

"Are we MOVING?" yelled Charlotte from the middle of the cave. She poked Dylan. "Wake up!"

The ground rolled beneath them. "Whoa," said Ling-Fei, crouching lower and moving away from the opening.

Billy got low to the ground and crawled toward her.

"Ling-Fei, what *exactly* did you ask the cave?" asked Billy.

"Last night, before I went to sleep, I told the cave that we wanted to get to the red dome and asked it to help us. I thought it might be sentient like the rock troll. And I guess it is!"

Billy crawled forward on his belly as close to the mouth of the cave as he dared and looked outside. "You're right," he said in awe. "The cave is . . . walking." It had sprouted long legs made of rock and was taking large steps. The entire cave swayed slowly from left to right in great sweeping motions. From what he could see, the earth was far below them.

The others slowly crawled toward Billy until they were lined up shoulder to shoulder, their heads poking out just past the edge of the entrance and peering down at the ground.

Ling-Fei patted the floor of the cave. "Thank you," she said. "You are a kind mountain."

"What do we do?" asked Dylan. He held his glasses with one hand to keep them from falling to the ground hundreds of feet below.

"I think we just have to wait it out," said Charlotte. "And hope Ling-Fei is right about where it's taking us."

After several hours, and the rest of the pork buns, the red dome came into view.

The walking mountain took them to the edge of the dark green and purple foliage surrounding the red dome, then slowly sank back down toward the earth. Billy and the others climbed out of the cave as soon as it settled on the ground.

"That was wild!" said Dylan, breathing heavily. He patted the various parts of his body, checking that he was still in one piece, before looking up. "And we survived!"

"Thank you again, friendly creature," said Ling-Fei.

"Yeah, thank you," said Charlotte with a curtsy.

"Seriously. The biggest thank you ever," added Billy.

"I never thought I'd be talking to a mountain, but, yes, thank you!" said Dylan.

The cave didn't respond, but Billy suspected it understood them.

They looked up at the red dome, towering above them. Eight plumes of purple smoke rose from within.

"What now?" whispered Dylan.

"We go in the red dome, and we find our dragons," said Billy. He could sense that Spark was close. He hoped she felt it too and that their dragons knew Billy and his friends were coming. "Then we stop Dimitrius and the Noxious from bringing back the Dragon of Death."

"Oh, sure, like it's that simple," said Dylan.

"Do you have any other ideas?"

"Oh, come on!" Charlotte whisper-shouted. "We're wasting time." She pushed ahead and tromped through the thick purple grass.

It was like entering an alien jungle. The grass rose to their knees, and giant purple trees blotted out the sun and stars above them. Prickly cactus-like plants grew all around, bearing strange black fruit on their spiky branches. As they passed an especially big cactus, one of the fruits fell and rolled toward Billy.

He leaned down and picked it up.

"I wouldn't touch that," said Dylan, backing up.

"Just checking it out," said Billy. "I'm not going to eat it or anything."

It had a fuzzy, sticky shell with bright purple veins covering its surface. It looked like an eggplant's evil twin.

Billy rapped on it. "Sounds hollow," he said. And then, exactly where he'd rapped, the fruit cracked open and hundreds of beetle-like insects poured out, crawling up Billy's arms and down his back.

"Ahhh!" yelled Billy, dropping the fruit. "Get them off! Get them off!" He frantically swatted at his arms and legs. The beetles had sharp pincers and pointy little legs, and he was terrified one was going to burrow into his skin. "Help me!"

Together Charlotte and Dylan swiped as many beetles off him as they could.

"What are these things?" Charlotte asked.

"I don't know," said Billy, "Just get them off!"

"I'm trying! I'm trying!" said Charlotte. "Stay still!"

"Watch out for the needles on the bushes!" cried Ling-Fei. "I'm getting a bad feeling about them!"

Billy swerved, but it was too late. One of the needles snagged on his palm. Blood welled instantly, and a stabbing pain shot from his palm all the way up to his neck.

"Guys," he said, staggering back. "I don't feel good."

His vision blurred, and his knees buckled.

"Billy!" Charlotte shouted, darting forward.

Billy reached out for her and then crumpled in a heap in the long grass.

CHAPTER 32
THE RED DOME

When Billy opened his eyes, the first things he saw were his friends' faces peering over him.

"He's not dead!" said Dylan.

"We knew he wasn't dead," snapped Charlotte. "He was breathing."

"How do you feel?" asked Ling-Fei.

Billy blinked and rubbed his eyes. "What . . . happened?" His brain felt fuzzy, and his head hurt.

"Oh, no, what if he has amnesia?" said Dylan. He got closer to Billy's face. "Do you know who I am?"

Billy sat up and pushed Dylan away. "I don't have amnesia," he said. "You are Dylan O'Donnell. We're in the Dragon Realm. But I don't remember what happened just now." He gestured around at the flattened grass where he'd landed.

"You opened that rotten fruit, which was a terrible

idea, then these horrible beetles came out of it, and then you panicked and ran into another plant that apparently was poisonous and knocked you out," said Charlotte.

"How long was I out for?"

"Just a few minutes," said Ling-Fei. "We didn't know what we were going to do if you didn't wake up!"

Billy looked around him and saw the purple spiky plants everywhere. He pointed at one. "That's what knocked me out? The needles?"

His friends nodded.

"Now I can sense that the plant has sleep-inducing properties," said Ling-Fei. "Sorry I missed it before. I was too focused on the red dome."

"Don't worry about it," said Billy. "We can't expect you to sense *everything* around you all the time." Then he started to grin. "I've got an idea."

After gathering as many of the needles as they could and putting them in Dylan's backpack, they carried on through the foliage toward the red dome, careful not to touch anything else. As they got closer, Billy saw that the dome looked as if it were breathing. Its translucent surface was covered in twisted red veins, and it rose and fell in a gentle rhythm.

"Do you think it's alive?" asked Dylan. "What are the chances this dome could attack us?"

"Ling-Fei?" asked Billy.

Ling-Fei tilted her head to the side, staring at the dome. "It feels . . . powered by something. But not alive. The whole thing stinks like dark magic. No wonder the evil dragons are called the Noxious." She wrinkled her nose.

"There's only one way to find out if this thing is going to kill us or not," said Charlotte. She reached out toward the dome. Her hand passed straight through, as if it were air. She pulled her hand back and inspected it. "It looks safe to me," she said as Dylan and the others joined her, examining the hand she was holding out. "The issue is that we can't get through here." Charlotte pointed back at the dome.

Directly on the other side of the translucent red surface was a solid limestone wall.

"You're right," Billy said. "We'll have to walk around the edge until we find an opening."

"Wait, look here!" said Ling-Fei, darting to the left and crouching low. "There's a small gap in the wall that we could crawl through."

"And we should have enough of those needles to knock out a dragon if we need to," said Charlotte.

"This feels like a deeply flawed plan," said Dylan dubiously. "We're just going to sneak around and try to get more information? With nothing to defend ourselves against the nox-wings except needles?"

"It's the only plan we've got," said Billy. "Come on, I'll go first."

Billy got down on his belly and army-crawled through the hole in the wall. The others followed. The air had a different quality inside the red dome. It was crackling like it had a static charge.

The tunnel was longer than Billy expected. His whole body was now snuggled into the crevice, and he couldn't see out of the other side. He held his breath, trying to work out if he could hear anything. Nothing. But he knew Spark was close. For the first time since they'd been separated, the bond felt stronger than a mere flicker.

After a few more minutes of wiggling through the tunnel, Billy saw a dim glow ahead. "We're almost there," he whispered over his shoulder. The closer he got to the inside of the dome, the more he felt the bond with Spark. But his joy at sensing his dragon quickly turned to fear. She was in pain. Billy wasn't sure if she was close enough to hear his thoughts, but he tried anyway. *We're coming, Spark. Just hold on.*

There was no response. Billy gritted his teeth and continued wriggling with new determination.

When he reached the end of the tunnel, he paused and listened again. Still nothing. He slowly emerged into the back of an enormous cavern. Charlotte, Ling-Fei, and Dylan came out behind him. There was a large pile of gold in front of them.

Billy held a finger to his lips and silently started to walk toward the cavern entrance.

Suddenly something rumbled up ahead, and a huge shape appeared from behind the pile of gold. It was an enormous maroon-colored dragon.

The four friends froze.

"Oh, no," moaned Dylan.

"Maybe it can't see us," whispered Charlotte.

The dragon whipped its head around and stared straight at them.

"Get the spikes out! Now!" said Billy, hoping his idea would work. If it didn't, they were dead.

Dylan fumbled with his backpack as smoke started to come out of the dragon's nostrils.

"You!" it roared, fire shooting out of its nostrils. "How did you get in here?" It flashed its teeth. "What a treat this is. I will feast on your small bones, and my fellow nox-wings will be pleased with me for getting rid of you bothersome children."

Billy knew that they only had one chance. "Now, Dylan!"

Dylan quickly handed a fistful of poisonous spines to Billy, careful not to prick either of their hands. Charlotte and Ling-Fei grabbed some, too.

"Throw!" said Billy.

A shower of poisonous needles fell on the maroon dragon and bounced off its scales.

"What's this?" said the dragon, amused. It picked up one of the needles and let out a laugh. "Silly humans! This mere plant can't pierce my armor."

Billy's heart sank into his stomach.

"Don't eat us!" yelled Dylan, making eye contact with the dragon.

"And why would I not eat four delicious humans?"

"Oh, well, we are highly poisonous beings. Didn't you know?"

The dragon blinked at Dylan a few times, clearly rolling what Dylan had just said around in its head.

Billy had an idea. He took the chance and dashed up to the dragon.

"Humans aren't poisonous," the dragon finally said. "Do not try to fool me."

Billy swept up a handful of needles from the floor before leaping toward the dragon's face. As Billy went to jab the spines into the dragon's eye, the dragon turned toward him, breaking free of Dylan's charm and swatting Billy out of the air. Billy flew into the dragon's hoard, sending gold coins in every direction.

The dragon roared and charged at Billy, its mouth wide. Billy fumbled around in the coins, trying to get away, but he couldn't move quickly enough. The dragon's jaws came closer and closer and suddenly snapped shut just short of Billy's face.

"I've got it!" cried Charlotte, holding the dragon back by its tail.

The dragon let out another frustrated roar, and as it did, Billy jabbed a handful of spines straight into its tongue and pulled away.

The dragon's roar turned to a sputtering cough, and then its head slumped to the side, and it collapsed on the ground with a thump.

"Let's go! Now!" said Billy. "We don't know how long that nox-wing will be out for!"

The group ran past the dragon and out the other side of the cavern, where the forest foliage continued under the dome. They raced to a line of trees and ducked low in the high grass.

"*That was madness!*" Dylan whisper-shouted. "I can't believe it worked!"

"But now we're out of weapons," said Charlotte. "We used all the needles!"

"Let's worry about that after we find Spark and the others," said Billy. "I know they are close. I can feel it. Can you guys?"

They all nodded.

"Look," said Billy, pointing through the trees toward the center of the dome. Up ahead was a clearing that crackled and flashed with electricity. "Let's get a better look. Stay quiet."

Billy led the way through the trees. Then he stopped suddenly, unable to believe what he saw.

There were hundreds of dragons. But that wasn't the shocking part.

The dragons were in cages.

CHAPTER 33
DRAGON HEARTS

The sight of the caged dragons made Billy feel sick. They weren't ordinary cages either. The bars buzzed and sizzled, seemingly made of electricity. Each cage was a different size, made to fit the dragon inside it—and around each dragon's neck was a tight collar made of the same electric material. The cages were positioned in a circle around a pulsing black hole that was swirling with electricity. Eight purple fires floated at various heights above the clearing, each giving off a plume of smoke.

Billy couldn't see Spark and the other dragons, but he knew they must be in there somewhere, having their life force drained.

When they had first arrived in the Dragon Realm and seen the dragon bones in the cave, he thought that was the worst thing that could happen to him and his friends. But now, feeling flashes of Spark's pain as her energy was sucked away, he wondered if the dragons in the cave had died merciful and quick deaths.

Having your life force drained felt like torture.

"Do you see that?" whispered Charlotte. "We have to release them! All of them! These must be the good dragons, the ones on our side, who survived."

Ling-Fei looked as though she might cry. Billy thought that he might. Seeing such majestic creatures confined like this and knowing how much pain they must be in, it was unnatural. It made his skin crawl. He still couldn't see Spark, but he could feel her agony through their bond even more now. It pulsed through him, strong enough to make him gasp.

"We are so out of our depth," said Dylan.

"This must be the portal they're creating to bring back the Dragon of Death," whispered Ling-Fei.

"I think you're right," said Billy, trying to focus even as another wave of pain came rolling in from his dragon bond. "We have to find our dragons. They're close; I can feel it."

"Look!" said Dylan, pointing. "They are in those cages over there!"

Billy looked up, and his heart jumped. Spark was staring right at him. With a sickening jolt, he realized how weak she had become since they'd been separated. Her eyes weren't the bright gold they had been when he last saw her. They were dimmer, faded. But as she kept her gaze on him, her eyes started to clear.

"We need to get closer," said Billy, but as he took his first step, the ground began to rumble. The portal in the center of the dome turned a dark, swirling violet. Then a crackling purple beam shot out from the portal up into the sky. Dark clouds formed around it, throwing everything in shadow.

There was the sound of beating wings up above. "Quick," said Billy. "Behind the trees!"

A moment later, Dimitrius and dozens of other nox-wings landed in a circle around the portal. Dimitrius roared triumphantly, waving his head from side to side, throwing a column of fire into the sky. "Nox-wings! We have done it! The portal is finally ready! We have enough life force to summon the Great One! Right at this very moment, she's making her journey back to our current time! Let it be known that we are the future of both the Dragon Realm and the Human Realm, and with the power that the Great One grants us, all shall fall under our rule."

Dimitrius and the nox-wings turned and gazed into the swirling portal, anticipating the Dragon of Death's imminent arrival.

"We need to get to our dragons!" Billy said. "Maybe they know how we can open their cages. And then we can fight the nox-wings and figure out a way to close the portal." He cut through the bushes toward Spark, with Charlotte, Dylan, and Ling-Fei following close behind. The nox-wings were so focused on the portal they didn't notice Billy and his friends sneaking by.

"Billy," said Spark quietly as they approached. "You came."

"Of course," said Billy. Spark's eyes glowed bright,

and Billy was filled with peace. Now that he was with Spark again, he felt like he could achieve anything.

"Thank you," said Spark. "We must act fast. Listen carefully, children. We are weak from having our life force drained, and we need you to be stronger than ever. Do you see those floating flames above us? Inside each one is a dragon's heart that has been possessed by dark magic, and that is what is draining our life force. Take the hearts out of the fire, and the cages will open. Once we are free, the portal won't have enough life force—"

A bolt of purple electricity shot toward them and wrapped around Spark's snout, sealing her mouth.

"Who are you talking to?" asked Dimitrius, thundering over.

Spark looked directly at Billy. *Jump, Billy,* she told him, and as soon as he did, blue frost shot out of Spark's nostrils, forming an ice board that slid right under him and latched to his feet. *You can control the board,* Spark told him. *Use our bond.*

Billy understood instantly. The ice board felt like it was part of him. Billy squatted down as if riding his surfboard, and he flew up toward the closest flame.

"Get the human children!" Dimitrius yelled, and he hurled a ball of fire at Billy.

Billy dodged to the left, the flame just missing him. Out of the corner of his eye, he saw more nox-wings coming at him. He dipped and dove as he flew into the air, dodging fireballs and ice boulders. As he approached the first purple flame, Billy thrust his arms in as fast as he could. Electricity buzzed through him, and then his hands closed on a wet, throbbing mass. He grabbed it and pulled. The fire immediately vanished, and the black beating heart in his hand burst into a cloud of ash.

"Nooooo!" yelled Dimitrius. "GET THAT BOY! And catch the escaped dragons!"

Billy looked down at Spark and saw that her cage and collar had vanished, as had the rope of electricity around her snout. She leapt into battle.

Stay focused, Billy, she thought. *I've got to help the others. With your power, you can maneuver better than any of us to destroy the hearts. Our bond is strong. It will keep you afloat. You can do this.* Spark's trust in Billy filled him with renewed energy.

The cages holding Buttons, Xing, and Tank disappeared too, the bolts of electricity sizzling as they went out. Charlotte, Ling-Fei, and Dylan ran to their dragons and jumped on their backs.

"Get all the dragon hearts!" Billy yelled to his friends. "The faster we get rid of the hearts, the more dragons we'll have on our side!"

Several of the nox-wings chasing Billy dove toward the ground to fight the newly released dragons. Billy raced to a second heart and ripped it from the flames, destroying more cages. Below him, the portal began to shrink.

The previously caged dragons and the nox-wings were fighting all around Billy now. Streams of fire and ice slashed through the air. Billy dipped and dodged on his floating ice board as he flew toward another heart.

"GET HIM!" yelled Dimitrius.

Billy zipped over a flying ice boulder and under a bolt of electricity, grabbing a third dragon heart.

"I've got one!" shouted Charlotte.

"Me, too!" yelled Dylan, looking triumphant as the black heart in his hands turned to ash.

"Take that!" cried Ling-Fei, grabbing a sixth heart.

Only two hearts remained.

Billy flew toward the next closest heart, dodging the fire coming at him from all directions. He could feel Spark through their bond, helping him guide the ice board.

"You will not succeed!" Dimitrius screamed from behind him.

Billy reached for the heart, but as he did, something struck the back of his ice board, smashing it to pieces. His momentum carried him through the air, and he tore the heart from the flames as he flew. But Dimitrius caught up to Billy as he fell and clutched him in his paw—his claws piercing through his protective suit.

Billy screamed. The pain was excruciating, and he was terrified. He was going to die. He would never see his parents or his brother again. He wished they could somehow know he died trying to save them, trying to save everyone.

"You shall pay for what you have done," said Dimitrius as he swooped toward the ground, holding Billy out in front of him. "You have no idea what you almost ruined."

Billy slammed into the earth with a thud, and pain shot through his whole body. It felt like every one of his bones had shattered. His vision blurred. He never knew he could feel such agony.

"Spark," he whimpered.

"Pitiful," said Dimitrius, his front leg pinning Billy to the ground.

Tank charged on the other side of the clearing, head-butting nox-wings out of the way, as Charlotte held on to his horns and screamed like a warrior queen, trying to get to Billy. Buttons and Dylan flew high above with Xing and Ling-Fei, dodging fire and ice and pelting the nox-wings with their own attacks.

Dimitrius reached up and plucked a star from the sky. "I am going to enjoy this," he said as he threw the star up toward his open jaws.

Billy saw a flash of blue and gold, and a familiar electricity buzzed through the air.

It was Spark! She had eaten the star. Within moments she had grown bigger than Dimitrius.

"Let him go!" she shouted, and she shot a jet of electricity at Dimitrius. He dodged the attack and fled upward, leaving Billy on the ground.

"Buttons! Come quickly!" Spark shouted, pulling Billy out of the fray. Billy heard a familiar hum as Buttons placed a giant paw gently on Billy's chest. "This might hurt," said Buttons. "Your body is very broken." As he spoke, a searing pain shot through Billy, making him feel like he was being melted from the inside out. His body went numb, and a moment later feeling slowly flowed back to his limbs.

"Billy, are you okay? You did great up there," said

Dylan, kneeling next to him. Charlotte and Ling-Fei were there as well.

A single purple flame remained, burning high above. Dragons continued to fight all around them.

Billy sat up gradually and looked at Dylan. "I . . . I think I'm fine." His voice shook. He couldn't quite comprehend that he had survived, but then his incredulity gave way to a fierce determination. He wasn't going to give up. He was going to keep fighting alongside his friends.

Dylan stood and offered a hand to help Billy up.

As Billy reached for Dylan's hand, a figure dashed out of the forest and grabbed Dylan. Dylan yelled as he was pulled away toward the center of the dome.

Billy flung himself to his feet, adrenaline rushing through him, and chased after Dylan. He thought at first it must be a rock troll or another Dragon Realm monster, but as he came closer, he realized it was a human.

And not just any human.

"Old Gold!" Billy shouted, still running after them. "Get back! It's dangerous." Billy's brain went into overdrive as he tried to work out what was happening. What was Old Gold doing here? How had he even found his way into the Dragon Realm? He must have read their notes and somehow followed them. But why had he grabbed Dylan? If Old Gold was trying to protect Dylan, he should be going back into the forest.

"Yeye!" shouted Ling-Fei. "What are you doing?"

Old Gold moved with intent, hurrying toward the closing portal.

But then he turned and gave Ling-Fei a nasty smile. It transformed his entire face, and Billy felt like he was looking at a stranger. A terrifying stranger. In one arm, Old Gold lifted a ball of purple electricity up to Dylan's face. His other arm held Dylan tightly in front of him like a shield. "Leave me be or the child dies!"

Billy halted immediately, horror spreading through him.

Old Gold looked back at Ling-Fei and sneered. "I'm not your yeye, you silly girl. How dare you keep that pearl from me? I killed your grandparents for the Lightning Pearl, and I would have killed you for the Jade Pearl! What a fool I was not to know you had it hidden in your necklace." Old Gold let out an unfamiliar laugh, his face barely recognizable.

Billy was so shocked, he couldn't move. He just stared at the man he thought he knew. The man he'd trusted. The man he'd thought was supposed to keep them safe. Next to Billy, Charlotte stared, openmouthed, and Ling-Fei was trembling like a leaf in the wind. Billy wanted to do something, anything, but it felt like his whole body was made of lead. He was frozen to the spot.

"I always knew children would be my way into the mountain," he said. "After all, who has a braver heart than a child? So brave. And so foolish." Old Gold moved closer to the portal. "Why do you think I wasted all that time setting up a ridiculous culture and language camp? I got as close as I could to the entrance. Oh, yes, I knew about Dragon Mountain from the oracle bones. It took me decades to work out what those bones said. And when I did, I tried everything. But I still couldn't get in! That infernal tiger kept chasing me away. And even when I realized it wasn't real, I couldn't get past it. But I knew I was close. I needed"—his lip curled—"four hearts. But that wasn't all. No, it was a matter of finding the right combination of hearts. The strange alchemy that would match all the desired traits of these dragons. The ones who would break the curse. But I had my own bits of magic, scavenged over the years. How do you think I found you brats in the first place? All it took was a little persuasion to convince your nitwit parents and teachers to send you to my camp."

Old Gold looked directly at Ling-Fei. "I'm glad I kept you alive all this time, although I'll admit I never thought you would be such a key part of this. Thank you for opening the mountain."

Old Gold surveyed the dragons surrounding them. "*I* will be the one to bring the Great One back. I will succeed where you have failed. I will not be denied. I have seen what glory the future holds for her and any others by her side, and I will stop at *nothing* to fulfill the Great One's vision. *I* will be the one to win her favor. *I* will be the one by her side when we rule both realms. All of you will bow to me. And the only being I shall answer to will be the Great One herself."

"You imbecile," said Dimitrius, who was still hovering above. He seemed to be watching all of this with amusement, Billy thought. "You need a dragon to travel through that portal."

Old Gold laughed again and flashed a vial of golden liquid in the hand holding Dylan. "And I do. I have the blood of the Great One herself, and it will take me straight to her! The portal may be too damaged for the Great One to return now, but we *will* return. Be prepared for the reckoning."

Old Gold still had the ball of purple electricity pressed against Dylan, whose face was frozen in terror. Billy willed him to fight back, to use his power against Old Gold, but Dylan appeared to have gone into shock. Billy wanted to rush forward and grab his friend, but he was terrified that if he got too close, Old Gold would carry out his threat and kill Dylan instantly.

"This one will come in handy," Old Gold said, jerking his head toward Dylan "You brats and your hearts seem to be good for opening doors. Who knows what else I can use him for?"

"No!" shouted Billy, a sickening realization dawning on him. But before he could do anything, Old Gold jumped into the portal, pulling Dylan with him. The portal closed behind them and disappeared.

CHAPTER 34
THE PROMISE OF A DRAGON

Billy stared at the ground where Dylan had been moments before.

A loud howl went up from Dimitrius. "Idiot human! He closed the portal! All our efforts for nothing! He will pay. You'll all pay! I will find the Great One. I won't be stopped."

Over a hundred good dragons, ones who had been caged, closed in on the nox-wings and Dimitrius. Bitter rage flashed across his face, and he flew high into the sky. The red dome had disappeared along with the portal. "You may outnumber us now, but this isn't over," he roared. "Noxious! To me!" With that, he and the rest of the nox-wings flew away.

Billy almost didn't hear any of it. He couldn't stop staring at the place where Dylan had disappeared with Old Gold. How could this have happened? He felt a stabbing guilt as he remembered that Dylan had wanted to turn back and Billy had convinced him to keep going. With everything they'd gone through together, Dylan had become one of Billy's closest friends. And now he was gone.

Billy squeezed his eyes shut, unable to face it all. He felt a nudge on his shoulder and opened his eyes. It was Spark. She had shrunk to her usual size. "I am so sorry, Billy."

Billy looked back down at the ground where Dylan had disappeared.

"We'll find a way to reopen the portal, right? We have to get him back." He looked around and realized the sun was shining. The dark clouds had cleared, revealing a bright blue sky. The three moons still sat across from the oval sun. Vibrant green grass was beginning to sprout rapidly from the earth, and the foliage at the edge of the clearing turned from deep shades of purple to a full range of greens, blues, reds, and yellows.

Billy didn't care about any of that. He only cared about his friends. Ling-Fei and Charlotte ran up to him. Ling-Fei had tears streaming down her face. Charlotte held Ling-Fei's hand. She was trembling with rage.

"I can't believe it," said Ling-Fei. "Old Gold really was like my yeye. I never even met my real yeye, because . . . because . . ." She couldn't even say the words.

"At least your yeye isn't a murderer," said a familiar voice from behind the trees. Billy spun around. It was JJ.

"What are you doing here? Were you helping Old Gold?" Billy wanted to shake JJ to get answers. He wanted to blame him for Dylan being taken. Deep down, he knew he wasn't being rational, but he didn't care. Billy hurt too much to be rational.

JJ stared at him with a dazed expression. "I don't even know where I am right now! Nothing seems real."

"JJ! Tell us what happened!" said Billy. The more information they had, the better chance they had of saving Dylan.

"We're listening," said Ling-Fei, wiping a tear from her cheek. "Please help us, JJ."

JJ took a deep breath, composing himself. "After you all ran off, my yeye started acting strange. He kept talking about dragons. And then he brought me to the mountain. He said he might need my heart, and I thought he meant he might need my help getting around or climbing over rocks. I didn't realize he literally meant my *actual heart*. He didn't tell me where we were going or what we were doing until we were in this place, and then he used some . . . some . . . sort of magic to get us from Dragon Mountain to here."

JJ looked around, fear all over his face. Billy suddenly remembered how terrified *he'd* been when he first saw their dragons. At least he'd had his friends with him. JJ had only had Old Gold, who had just jumped into a time portal and abandoned him. He must be even more frightened than Billy had been. Billy tried to swallow his anger and frustration. JJ really did seem to be completely unaware of Old Gold's evil plan.

"I feel like I never even knew him," JJ said. "He turned into a different person."

"Do you think he'll hurt Dylan?" asked Billy.

JJ looked down at the ground again. "I don't know," he said. "He really wants to find that dragon he keeps calling the Great One. I think he'd do anything to get to her."

"Well, we're going to find Dylan, and you are going to help us," said Billy fiercely.

"Billy is right," said Xing, who had flown over. The rest of the recently released good dragons gathered close, surrounding the children.

"They will not get away with this," said Tank.

"We will find a way to save Dylan," said Spark. "I promise. And the promise of a dragon is an unbreakable thing."

One of the dragons at the back gave a supportive roar. Others followed.

Soon, all the dragons in the clearing were roaring in unison. When they finally quieted down, a long serpentine dragon approached Billy and Spark. The dragon looked very similar to Xing except its scales were gold instead of silver. "All is not lost. Thanks to you we are free, and the life force that was being used to open the portal has flowed back to us and the land. With your help and your bravery, we have reclaimed the Dragon Realm and restored it to health. You can see that everything around you is turning back to its original form right before our eyes. And now we will have enough power on our side to defeat Dimitrius and the nox-wings. Dimitrius tricked us and used dark magic to trap us, but now we are free, and we won't be fooled again. We owe you a great debt."

Billy found he didn't care. They'd lost Dylan. That was all that mattered now. "Then you'll help us find

Dylan?" asked Billy. He couldn't imagine how scared Dylan must be, how alone he must feel. He knew in that moment he'd do anything to save his friend. To bring him back.

"Of course," said the gold dragon. "It is the least we can do."

"Then it's settled," said Tank. "We'll find a way to track down Dylan and Old Gold."

"I know how to find them," said a morose voice from behind them. It was Buttons.

"Buttons!" said Billy, running to him. He knew Buttons must be in agony at being separated from his human. As painful as Billy found Dylan's kidnapping, it would be much worse for Buttons. "Are you all right?"

Buttons closed his eyes, and his face drooped. "It feels . . . like I've been sundered in two. Like a piece of me is missing."

"Buttons, if you can feel the pain," said Spark gently, "that's a good sign."

"Yes, I know," said Buttons. He opened his eyes to look at the children. "It means Dylan is still alive. And that the bond is able to stretch through time itself."

A slow understanding dawned on Billy. He looked up at his friends and at their dragons.

"We're going to have to go through time to save Dylan," he said. "And to stop the Dragon of Death."

"It will be hard," warned Tank.

"And dangerous," added Xing.

"It doesn't matter," said Billy, his exhaustion and fear giving way to a burning determination. "It'll be worth it.

No matter what it takes."

Ling-Fei stepped forward. "I'm in," she said.

"Me, too," said Charlotte.

Billy picked up Dylan's backpack and put it on. "Let's go and find Dylan."